Christine

PONY PATROL

Illustrated by Jennifer Bell

SIMON & SCHUSTER

LONDON • SYDNEY • NEW YORK • TOKYO • SINGAPORE • TORONTO

First published in Great Britain in 1991
by Simon and Schuster Young Books

Photoset in North Wales by
Derek Doyle & Associates, Mold, Clwyd.
Printed and bound in Great Britain by
The Guernsey Press Co. Ltd,
Guernsey, Channel Islands.

Simon and Schuster Young Books
Simon and Schuster Ltd
Wolsey House
Wolsey Road
Hemel Hempstead HP2 4SS

British Library Cataloguing in Publication Data
Pullein-Thompson, Christine
    Pony Patrol.
    I. Title   II. Series
    823.914 [F]

ISBN 0 7500 0805 9
ISBN 0 7500 0806 7 (pbk)

Contents

Chapter One

Why did it happen to us?

William stood alone, his eyes smarting from the smoke, his face blackened by it. He looked at his parents and knew suddenly that they were all older because of what had happened, much older. It wasn't only because they had lost thousands of pounds worth of hay and straw. It was the work which had gone into producing it too, the hours spent labouring in the fields from dawn till near midnight with aching arms. His father was still in his pyjamas under an old coat and was wearing Wellington boots. He was weeping and William had never seen him weep before. Sometimes people called him a hard man, but he was not hard now, standing and weeping while dawn came quietly above the smouldering barns. His mother was in the house putting the kettle on, older and sadder and more harassed than ever. The firemen were putting out the last of the smouldering straw. They looked tall and dramatic in the gathering dawn.

William had raised the alarm, had heard the roof of the Dutch barn exploding like gunfire in the heat of the burning straw underneath. He had rushed down the stairs yelling "Fire!", smelling the smoke before he saw the flames. Outside he had found a blazing inferno. The old barn was alight too, its wooden sides cracking and splintering. As he stood appalled, the roof had fallen in. And the barn had stood there for six hundred years! He had remembered the horses then, and had run to the stable beyond, pulling them out of their boxes by their forelocks, chasing them into the thirty-acre field beyond.

His mother had rung for the fire engine. His father had fetched buckets of water and thrown them at the blaze but without hope, and it was then that he had started to cry like an old man.

The police had come now. They were questioning his father, looking at William as though he had started the blaze.

"No trouble there," his father said. "We get on well enough, William and myself."

His mother was giving the firemen mugs of tea, wondering whether to offer the policemen some too. The horses stood on the hill ringed by the rising dawn, their grey socks and stars standing out in the blackness of the fading light. The grey, Boxer, had his ears up, his nostrils quivering. They were all ready to flee, their muscles taut.

A policeman was asking him if he smoked. "No never," William said. "Not near the barns anyway. Ever! I'm a farmer's son." It sounded pompous, but it wasn't meant to be. It was just the truth. He knew too much to smoke near stables or hay or straw. He wasn't a townie. He had grown up here among the flat fields crossed by dykes, fringed by tremendous trees of great beauty.

"It's a complete mystery," said his father wearily.

Some of the police were prodding the smouldering hay, searching outside the remains of the barn for some sort of clue.

William saw in his mind the long winter starting. It was September already and the fields were parched from a long dry summer. What would the animals eat now? he wondered. The three hundred head of cattle, the horses? He saw their ribs showing through their long winter coats, the poverty marks growing deeper every day on the horses' quarters.

"It's not the first hay and straw to go up tonight. There's an arsonist around," a policeman in a peaked cap said.

An arsonist was someone who set fire to things, who liked fire, who was mad or vicious, William knew that.

"Or two or three," another policeman said.

"But why did it happen to us?" his mother asked.

"Have you any enemies?" They were all going towards the house now. They were going to take down statements. The fire was out, the drama over, the terrible damage done.

"Not that I know of. I've sacked a man or two in my time, though. I had the right. There was one that stole, another who beat up the horses. And another who was just plain dirty, who kept the cottage like a pigsty," replied William's father.

And William remembered them – big dour men, and a small one with the sharp face of a rat. They had gone angrily, shouting over their shoulders, abusing them all.

"It's the third farm to go up in three days," a fireman said. "If you've got any straw left, I advise you to guard it night and day."

"So it's not just us being got at for something?" William asked.

"Not by a long way."

The firemen had finished. There was no longer a spark to be seen, just heaps of black and broken beams, twisted metal and the dreadful smell which hung over everything, a smell William would never forget.

"Tell your friends to watch their hay and straw, night and day, I mean it," the fireman continued.

"Thank you," William said. "Thank you very much." And as he spoke an idea was growing, an idea which meant he would be fighting back, would be doing something to avenge such pointless destruction. Names flashed through his mind. Names like Amanda, who had been hurt too. The Doyles who were ready for anything. Marvin . . .

He saw them all riding at night, watching, searching, investigating, until at last they caught the culprits, and dragged them to the police. He could feel excitement growing inside him like a rising river. He was not going to weep like his father, he was going to fight back. He would never give in. He felt better now. He wished that morning had really come so that he could be on the telephone organizing the patrols which he saw in his mind's eye riding out each night. They would have to have a name – the Pony Squad, or Legion, or even the Pony Brigade. They would not be searching for the arsonists alone. There were plenty of other dreadful things happening in the depths of the night. He saw himself leading the squad on dear, wise Boxer, who would jump anything and go for ever without getting tired. He

9

saw a host of riders following him. Would they carry weapons? He didn't know yet. The fire engines were leaving now, the firemen weary and silent. The policemen were coming out of the house. He could smell bacon frying. There was no point in going back to bed, because morning had almost come now. Another hour and it would be milking time.

The police stopped to question him, to ask him about school.

"Have you any enemies? Do you take drugs? Do you get on with your parents?" They seemed pointless questions to him. Of course he had enemies. He called them yobs. They were boys who never worked, who ruined the lessons and kicked the younger boys around. But they would not set fire to the barns; they were not that bad. He had never taken drugs either, though he had been offered them; and as for his parents, they were all right. He had arguments with them like everybody else of his age. But if the police thought he would set fire to the barns to get his own back, they must be mad. He tried to be polite, but all the time he was seeing his squad going out night after night, returning at dawn, beating the police at their own game. He could hear their hoofs on the roads and across the empty stubble-fields, the horses blowing, hushed voices. He would return at milking time. He would fall asleep at school, but to hell with school, there were some things more important than education, in his opinion anyway.

To the police he looked tall and sullen with dark hair smelling of smoke, steady blue eyes and a mouth with scorn in it, which didn't smile. They couldn't know that his mind was far away, that to him their questions were completely stupid.

Later he had breakfast, and then it was half-past-six and the first cows were starting to come in from the fields followed by Pete, who lived five miles away and came to work on a moped.

"I will ring Amanda first," he thought. "She gets up early and she's known trouble too. She will have lots of suggestions." He had known her a long time. They had been to Pony Club Camp together, hunted together. She was broad shouldered and quiet and, in his mind, utterly dependable.

Chapter Two

A sort of riding club

It was a long time before anyone answered. William stood in the small dark hall waiting. Daylight had come now, a misty September morning, in spite of the promising dawn. He had eaten bacon and eggs in the stone-floored kitchen while his mother talked, going over and over the horror of the fire, asking again and again. "Why us? What have we done to deserve it? Who have we ever harmed?"

Until at last William had said, "It's a madman. He's not connected with us. He's doing it to other people too. Can't you understand?"

But she did not want to understand, she was convinced it was someone with a personal vendetta against them.

Amanda answered the telephone at last. She sounded half asleep.

"Who is it? What's happened?" she asked resentfully. William imagined her standing in her parents' bungalow in a dressing-gown.

"I need your help. It's me," he said.

"Me?"

"William."

"What's happened? Have your horses been stolen?" Amanda asked, sounding more awake.

"Our hay has all gone, and the straw, burnt down by a lunatic or someone." He was trying to keep his voice steady, but it would not stay steady. He could not get over the awfulness of what had taken place.

There was a pause as the words sank in and then Amanda asked, "Oh, no! Not really. But why?"

"We don't know."

"Not all of it?"

"Yes, and the old barn too."

"But it had a conservation order on it. What are you going to feed your animals on?"

"Don't ask me." In an awful way he was enjoying the drama of breaking the news, and hating the enjoyment at the same time.

"You know what it's like. You had Tango stolen. You know how it feels to lose something, don't you?' he asked.

She said, "Yes," glancing behind her through the window at the empty box which had once housed beautiful Anglo-Arab Tango. She had never stopped searching for her. Whenever she saw horses turned out in a field she had to look to see whether he was among them. She knew it was worse losing him, than the effects of the fire, because there would be other crops of straw and hay, but never another Tango.

She could hear her mother getting up now, and there was light coming through the heavy damask curtains drawn across the sitting-room window. . .

William was still talking. He sounded gruffer, older, as though his voice had broken in the night. "I want to form a squad, a sort of patrol. These madmen are going to set fire to other barns, do lots more damage. I want us to catch them. I want justice done." His throat was aching from the smoke he had swallowed. He felt tired suddenly. He wished it was night instead of morning so that he could sleep.

"I want lots of people. Will you join, and what about the Doyles? I know it's school soon, but not yet, there's still a week left and more for people who go to private schools. We can ride out every night at twilight,' he said.

"I'll join of course," she answered. "But what about our parents? They will have to agree?"

"After all, you're thirteen and I'm nearly fifteen. We're nearly grown up. And anyway law and order has broken down. We are back in the old days when there were horse thieves. We need dogs and guns, but we will manage without . . ." William said.

"Supposing there's a fight?"

"We will use our fists." He was tired, but he knew that he would not rest until everything was arranged. Then he would have a few hours' sleep, before the patrol set out.

"There's Marvin," she said.

"I'll contact the Doyles too," William said.

"And there's the Merriots," Amanda added. "Or do you think they are too rich? I mean Leon is sure to come in a cloak with a silver gun or something."

"He'll do," William said. "They must all be here at three o'clock in the barn. Okay?" he asked.

"But it's burnt down," she said gently.

"In the stable then. Okay?"

"Okay."

"Who was that?" asked Amanda's mother, when she had replaced the receiver.

"Just somebody – William. His barns have been

burnt down, all of them." She had the telephone directory in her hand now. No one had mentioned a horse for her. William had forgotten that she had nothing to ride. Her mother was picking up the mail. She wasn't horsey and didn't really understand.

"Can they buy some more?" she asked, fluffing up the sitting-room cushions.

"I don't know. There isn't much about, most of it has gone to Cornwall this year," Amanda replied.

Her father was getting up now, going to the bathroom, turning on the taps. It was like any other morning except that William had rung up, and now they were starting something which could take them anywhere, which could lead to death, injury, anything. Amanda wished that her mother would go away so that she could use the telephone unheard. She thought, "It might even lead us to Tango, one never knows."

William was ringing up the Doyles. Emily answered. She was nine and always tried to reach the phone first. "Headly 305. Emily Doyle speaking. Who is that?" she gabbled.

"William Gaze. Can I speak to one of your sisters?" he asked.

The Doyles lived in a large, old, untidy house. They could never find anything, because it was always lying under something else. The window shelves were piled high with letters which needed answering and bills which needed paying. Mrs Doyle wrote articles for newspapers under several different names. Nobody really knew what Mr Doyle did, not even his children. They had three ponies, which lived in a tangled unpruned orchard and grew ill on fallen apples. In the winter the ponies ate the bark off the trees so every summer there were a few less trees.

Trudy came to the phone. "I was in bed. What is it?" she asked.

"We've had a fire. Someone has burnt our barns down. There are men setting fire to hay and straw. They are mad. We've got to catch them," William said, and knew that he was sounding mad himself, because he was tired and didn't know how to put his idea into words any more. "Have you any hay or straw?" he asked.

"No, not yet. We haven't got round to buying any yet. Mum is waiting for a cheque from a newspaper. Then we are going to buy lots."

"There won't be any to buy soon," replied William. "I'm organizing a pony patrol to try and catch the arsonists. We're having a meeting here this afternoon in the stable, three sharp. Will some of you come along?" He could never remember how many Doyles there were, so he added, "Not Emily, she's too young. But everyone else."

"Except Minnie?"

"Who's Minnie?"

"The baby," laughed Trudy.

"Come by horse if you can. We want a good line-up. We'll need two squads if possible. When do you go back to school?"

"I don't know. Do you want me to try to find out?"

"No, don't bother." He rang off, and wished he knew how many Doyles were coming and how old they were.

Marvin was out when William phoned the small renovated cottage where he lived, but his mother knew about the fire.

16

"The blaze lit up our windows in the night. Marvin wanted to go over to you, but I thought he would get in the way. And the smoke would have started up his asthma," she said.

"That's all right, Mrs George, just ask him to be here at three o'clock, mounted please."

"Right you are, William, and I'm ever so sorry; if there's anything I can do. I mean anything." She was going to talk for hours, and he didn't want to talk. He wanted to sleep for a bit and forget the horrors of the night. He kept saying, "Thank you. Yes, thank you very much," without really listening.

He could hear the tractor going out now, which meant his father was taking fodder down to the cattle in the bottom meadow, but what fodder? He should be helping.

He said, "Thank you, thank you ever so much," and hung up.

Outside the mist was beginning to clear and he knew that it was to be another scorching day, when all they wanted was rain.

"Your father has had a rest. Go and have one yourself, just for twenty-minutes," his mother said.

Later, two miles away, Amanda was ringing up Marvin too, explaining about the tragedy, saying, "Will you join the squad, please?" Marvin was standing in his parents' cottage wondering whether he would get on with William, wondering whether he was the tallest now.

"We are meeting at three o'clock at William's farm," Amanda said. "Bring Skinflint along. Please. After all you don't want your hay burnt."

"No one would find it. It's hidden behind the

garage. All right, I'll come," Marvin said.

The Merriots were at home too. Leon answered. He made silly remarks and then offered to arm them all with antique weapons. Amanda kept saying, "Please be sensible. You've got a farm too."

"But we don't farm it," he said.

"But you'll want the hay for your horses."

"Fair enough," he said, standing in the magnificent hall of his parents' magnificent house, clutching the emerald-green telephone receiver. "You've scored a point there."

Amanda wanted to scream, "It isn't a game, with points and marks, not snakes and ladders." But she didn't. She said, "You'll come then, and bring your sister won't you? Both mounted? Three o'clock at Deep Wood Farm. Okay?"

"Without a doubt," he said.

She rang off quickly before he could say anything more. And her mother, sniffing like a hound hunting something, asked, "You're not doing anything silly, are you? Not organizing a party or anything?"

"No," Amanda replied. "Just a sort of riding club."

Chapter Three

A meeting

The Doyles came first on their round grubby ponies. Trudy was riding a dun with a loose shoe. She had fair hair and a turned-up nose and was wearing jeans and an open-necked shirt. Her sister Alice was riding a roan called Mickey Mouse. He had straight pasterns and a straight shoulder, but was a hundred per cent reliable. They were twins and nearly twelve. Following them came Helen on her new bay. She was thirteen and tidier than the others. She had cleaned her tack and put on jodhpurs. They tied their ponies to the iron-railed yard where the cows waited to be milked at milking time. Everything still smelt of fire and smouldering straw. William came out of the house with a mug of coffee in his hand, his eyes still smarting from the smoke.

"It's awful," Helen said. "And the barn was so lovely too. It makes you want to cry."

William had put chairs out in the yard, stiff-backed dining-room chairs. He said, "Do sit down. The others must be here soon."

"Emily wanted to come, but we managed to leave her behind," Trudy told him. "She screamed her head off, of course, and Mum was furious."

Amanda arrived next on her bike, her hair windblown. "I've brought paper and pencil," she said, dismounting, "in case we want to write anything down." She went across to the Doyles' ponies and started patting them, and William said, "I'll find a mount for you, Amanda. Don't worry about having no horse."

"We will look for Tango too, won't we?" she asked.

"Yes, but she's not likely to be near here," William said.

Marvin arrived next on his show pony, which was a chestnut called Skinflint, with a star.

"I can't tie him up," he said. "He must have a box. I'm sorry."

"Follow me," William said. He felt older than any of them now, it was something to do with the fire; he couldn't explain why or how – it had simply happened.

The stables were old-fashioned cart-horse stalls turned into loose-boxes. There were twelve altogether.

"Great. Thanks," Marvin said. He had red hair and freckles and was supposed to be clever. His parents were ambitious for him and he was always being coached for something. He was expected to win at shows and be first in his class at school – to be first at everything. The strain showed on his face.

"Here comes Leon," shouted Amanda.

Leon rode into the yard now on his large bay which was called Flaming Prince, followed by his sister Natasha, who rode a beautifully turned out skewbald called Checked Princess – Checky for short. They wore beautifully cut trousers and silk shirts.

"Follow me to the loose-boxes," William said, feeling suddenly smaller and shabbier.

And so now at last they were all there – the three Doyles, Amanda, Marvin, Leon, Natasha and William – eight in all.

William fetched another chair. "I was going to put out bales of straw until I realized there weren't any left," he said.

"Pity you cut it so early," Leon replied. "We've still got another twenty acres to cut."

"Dad can never wait. He was afraid of rain, he always is," William replied, looking at the cloudless sky.

"You had better watch yours," Amanda told Leon.

"I want to start riding out tonight. Is that possible?" William asked. "How many of you can come?"

"All of us," replied Trudy Doyle. "Our parents are out. They are taking Minnie with them. We are as free as the air." She was laughing now, half falling off her chair with excitement.

"Just name the time," cried Alice, giggling. "I hope there's a moon."

"Someone has taken all our neighbour's ducks. It could be a thief, or it could be a fox," Helen said. "Can we ride that way too?"

"Okay," William said, wishing they would be more serious.

"I can manage it, but can it be eleven or later? My parents go to bed at ten," Marvin asked. "I'll have to creep out unseen."

"I'll say I'm spending the evening here," Amanda

said. "I can say I'm staying the night in your spare room, is that all right?"

"Yes. My parents know about us," William said. "They don't mind. Yes, stay the night, only it may not still be night when you get back."

"Our parents are in town," said Natasha, in her posh voice which set William's teeth on edge. "We can cope with Nanny. She believes anything we say, doesn't she, Leon?"

Her brother nodded. "No trouble there," he said. He wore his fair hair in a smart bob and went to one of the most expensive schools in England. "Do we carry guns?" he asked.

"Better not," said William.

"There could be an accident," answered Amanda. They were both a little afraid of Leon; they never knew how he would react to anything. They had known him for several years and yet sometimes they didn't think they knew him at all.

"Let's meet at midnight outside The Hare and Hounds," suggested William. "All mounted, with useful things like penknives, money and pieces of string, but no guns."

"And we'll be the Pony Patrol," said Helen.

"Yes," shrieked the twins.

Suddenly the air was electric with excitement and they were all imagining the night; and they knew that nothing would stop them now – they would ride out whatever happened, even if it meant climbing down drainpipes to get out of their bedrooms unnoticed.

"We are going to look for horse thieves, too," said Amanda with a catch in her voice.

"Of course," agreed William, looking at them with satisfaction. They are a mixed lot, he thought,

23

but they all have courage and that's what will count, when all the chips are down and we meet the arsonists face to face.

They all stood up, saying, "Tonight then."

They mounted their ponies and rode away, making plans and talking, while William and Amanda walked up a sloping meadow to look at the horses.

"I'm so large, I have to ride Boxer, but you can have any of the others," William said. He had always liked Amanda. He didn't like girls with airs and graces and ribbons in their hair, and she had none. She was what his mother called "Down to earth, with bags of common sense."

"There's Willow, he's reliable," he said pointing to the dun. "Or there's Dad's old hunter, Mulberry, or Suzy, who I rode in the Prince Philip competition last year."

"She's the fittest, isn't she? The others haven't been ridden for ages, have they? Can I have her then?" Amanda asked.

"Okay," William had his arm round Boxer now.

"I will be round about nine then to get her ready," Amanda said. "Thanks a million."

Suzy was a neat little grey with a head which pulled at your heart-strings. She was fast and handy and would tie up anywhere.

"She's not a hundred per cent in traffic, that's the only thing," said William, as they walked back towards the farm and Amanda's bike. "You'll have to watch it."

"I will. Don't worry. Tango wasn't a hundred per cent either."

"I hope everything goes all right. I hope we catch them."

"So do I." She was riding away now on her bike. William went indoors imagining the empty night. What if we run into the police? he thought. What will they say? Will they send us packing? And what about the horses? Supposing it's a pitch-black night? What then? We'll have to carry torches, stirrup lights . . . Why didn't I think of that before? He had a choking feeling in his throat now, a sick feeling in his stomach. If anything goes wrong it will be my fault, fair and square, no argument, he thought, because I thought of it. He wanted to whistle, but suddenly he couldn't. For the first time he saw difficulties ahead, perhaps disaster. At the same time he knew that nothing would stop them going now. It was a challenge and they had accepted it. There would be no turning back. He thought of the Doyles and suddenly they seemed too young. He thought of Marvin and his show pony which wasn't made for adventures in the night and had cost over two thousand pounds, and suddenly he realized how much he was responsible for. His mother had a mug of tea waiting for him. He drank it without tasting anything.

"What's the matter, son?" she asked.

"Nothing, just leave me alone," he answered, rushing upstairs.

His room was at the top of the house so that he could make as much noise as he liked without upsetting his parents. There were clothes on all the chairs, books everywhere, his riding boots on his bed. He put on his radio and thought, if only it was midnight already. But outside the sun still shone, drying up the grass, turning the leaves yellow, when they should still be green.

The cows were coming in to be milked now, the farm dog following them, yapping at their heels.

"Please let everything be all right tonight," prayed William. "And please let us catch those villains, *please*."

Chapter Four

Too late

Amanda and William were first there, waiting outside the low flint-built pub in the uncertain moonlight. Amanda had oiled their horses' hoofs. Boxer stood wise and alert, listening for hounds.

"He thinks we're cub hunting. We meet here sometimes," William said. His fears had gone now that he was mounted. It was always like that with him – once on a horse, anything seemed possible, anything at all.

Suzy danced a little, jingling her bit between her teeth. She seemed to match the moonlight, white and dappled, prancing like the moon. The pub behind them was in darkness, the sign creaking, and quite near, a dog was barking. Then the Merriots came riding down the road, Leon leading. He was wearing his cross-country helmet with a spotted silk over it. He tapped it as he arrived, saying, "I reckon it might stop the bullets."

Natasha's red-gold hair flowed over the collar of a yellow sweater. She had left her hat at home. More hoofs were coming now, and they could hear curtains being drawn back in the pub. Another minute and an old woman looked out. Her voice was weak and querulous. "What are you doing here?" she demanded.

"It's a midnight steeplechase," replied Leon instantly, without batting an eyelid.

Marvin was trotting towards them now, Skinflint shying at everything, enjoying himself.

The old woman shut the window with a bang.

"My parents wouldn't go to bed. It was awful. Am I late?" he called.

"Only two minutes," William replied, looking at his watch. Then a church clock chimed the hour and they laughed and said, "You're dead on time," and excitement mounted and the horses sensed it and pawed the ground, and shook their heads.

The Doyles were coming now, their ponies' hoofs clattering on the road, quick pony hoofs. They were arguing, shrieking at each other and there were four of them.

"We had to bring Emily. She woke up. We couldn't leave her alone in the house. She *would* come," Trudy called.

"She screamed and screamed," added Alice.

"You *know* Emily!" added Helen.

"She'll be nothing but a liability," grumbled William.

"Mickey Mouse will look after me. Why should I always miss everything?" shouted Emily.

Trudy was riding a bay with white socks called Dumpling. He was gone in the wind and made a snorting noise.

William thought, everything's going wrong. I can sense it. Emily is just the beginning.

"We had better split up," he said. "You're the eldest, so will you lead one group, Leon? I thought we would do a broad sweep and meet back here at about two, one of us going down Parson's Lane, the other over the thicket and across Highdown Hill."

"You can have the Doyles then," Leon said.

"And Amanda?"

"That will leave me with only three of us," retorted Leon.

"Oh, all right. You have Amanda and we'll change it round tomorrow," William said. "I'll go over Highdown Hill."

"I'm not a parcel," Amanda said grumpily.

They didn't dare split up the Doyles because their ponies were used to one another and could never be parted.

Inside himself William boiled with fury against Leon's bossiness. Outwardly he said, "Check your girths," and pulled up his own.

The thicket was short and thick and beyond was open land with a view which stretched for miles.

"Stick by me, Emily," Helen said. "Keep your heels down."

"We aren't going to gallop are we?" asked Emily.

For a moment the moonlight had gone and there was nothing but the thicket, damp with spiders' webs, prickly with thorns. There were rabbits everywhere and the occasional cry of a bird. Then the moon appeared again, and they could see the landscape below, lovely and remote.

William didn't feel like talking. He was angry with Leon for having Amanda with him. He started to trot, Boxer's hoofs eating up the miles, the ponies scurrying along in their efforts to keep up. They saw a monk jack, and the brush of a fox moving swiftly through the thicket, and then they were in the open with moonlight everywhere and cattle grazing on wiry grass. They stopped and stared then, standing in their stirrups, and the ponies grazed while Boxer stood still, listening for the cry of hounds.

"It's one o'clock," said William, looking at his watch. "We'd better go on, there's Hatch Gate Farm down at the bottom and that could be a target for the arsonists.

He was filled with gloom now, sure that nothing would happen. And the Doyles sensed it and were silent. "Only three more days to school," he thought, "and then nothing but talk about exams, homework, new teachers, new pupils. Another year."

Hatch Gate Farm dreamed in the moonlight. A man stood by the Dutch barns with a gun in his hand.

"What do you want? Oh, it's you, is it, William? That's all right then. Seen anything of them?" he asked.

"Nothing yet," William answered, "but we are watching. We'll have them if they strike tonight."

"Good boy." The man was a friend of his father's. He stood eyeing Emily, doubtless thinking that she was a bit small for such an expedition.

"Well, 'bye for now." William turned Boxer, and the Doyles followed, talking in undertones to one another, arguing about something or other. He started to canter slowly, wondering where the others were, his ears sifting every sound, suddenly unexpectedly happy. They reached a hill on the other side of the farm and the moon was still shining, though now there was a feeling of dawn in the air. They stopped and stared down into another valley, and then suddenly Emily cried, "Look!

Look over there! Look!" her voice rising to a scream of excitement, and they saw the outline of a barn and a trickle of fire, and Trudy yelled, "It's Leon's barn," and suddenly they were all galloping, the blood racing through their veins, with no other thought in their heads but the spreading fire below.

William couldn't have said afterwards how many things he jumped. They came and went, banks, a wall, rails, dykes. He forgot the Doyles. He became part of Boxer and Boxer became part of him, knowing how urgent the gallop was, straining every muscle to cross the moonlit landscape. Rabbits fled at their approach, while the fire grew brighter until soon it was lighting up the other buildings down below, a mere three fields away now, great golden stubble-fields full of fleeing pheasants.

He thought he heard a scream once, but it hardly registered in his brain. He remembered the barns at home burning and now he could hear the same sounds, the roofs going off like gun fire as they cracked in the heat, and he thought, we are too late, and could feel tears of grief and anger smarting behind his eyes.

Two miles away the other half of the patrol had seen the fire and were galloping too. Leon had seen it first and shouted, "It's our barn!" He had turned his horse and ridden as though to battle. Natasha followed, riding elegantly, her legs in the right position, her hands in the right place. Thoughts ran through her swiftly like a cool river. She knew, with a deadly certainty, that her father would be overcome with rage, because he loved money more than almost anything else on earth, and the straw

in his barns was worth thousands of pounds. She knew that he would shout at them, blame her brother somehow, whatever happened, and with a frightening feeling of cold despair, she knew already that they were too late. She knew too that what had been started as a sort of game was now something far more important. She seemed suddenly to be facing up to the bad side of life for the first time.

Suzy wasn't really fit. Amanda could feel her tiring already. She thought, it won't hurt the Merriots to lose their fodder, they have enough money to buy another million tons; Suzy's wind is more important than their barn. She drew rein and Marvin slowed down too, saying, "We're too late by about fifteen minutes. Damn."

Skinflint was not used to crossing the landscape at such a pace, and his neck was lathered with sweat, his reins slippery with it, his sides going in and out like bellows. If Mum saw him now she would have a fit, Marvin thought.

Leon galloped through a wood and was on home ground now and could see the farm manager beating at the fire with a stick and Nanny leaning out of a window screaming and men running – Jim and old Hermann and the new hand, Andy.

They heard sirens in the distance next, and then along the road which wound through distant stubble-fields like a snake, they saw police cars racing, their flashing blue lights hardly showing in the moonlight.

William reached the fire first. He halted Boxer and slipped off, leaving him to stand blowing while he ran towards the blaze yelling. "Can I do anything to help?" though he knew the answer already – he was too late.

He could hear the Doyles chattering behind, still crossing the stubble, and he could hear the wail of police sirens.

The farm manager was still in his pyjamas. "I was sitting up. I had my gun," he said. "I must have dropped off."

They had a hose now, connected to the farmhouse tap, dousing the flames, and another from the dairy. They were better organized than William's father had been. But it wasn't enough – most of the straw was burnt and half the hay in the next barn was beginning to crackle, sending up sparks in all directions. And now the police had arrived, leaping out of their cars, running here, then there looking for clues, talking into their radios, setting up road blocks.

Then Natasha and Leon came, and Nanny, in a dressing-gown screamed. "Where have you been? You and Natasha?"

As if it mattered now, thought William.

"I don't know what your father will say, I really don't," she went on, while Natasha sat weeping on Checked Princess.

Then Trudy started to scream, 'Where's Emily? We haven't got her. She's not here!"

And Alice yelled. "I forgot she was with us!"

And Helen said in a horribly quiet voice, "She couldn't possibly have jumped those jumps." William said, "I thought she was with you. We'd better look for her," remounting Boxer, as two fire engines raced into the yard. "I told you she

34

shouldn't have come. I told you not to bring her," he said.

"She's probably dead somewhere by now," said Trudy, bursting into tears.

Chapter Five

Where are you?

They all started to call, "Emily! Emily, where are you?" And the empty fields echoed their voices and brought them back.

"Mum will never forgive us," wailed Alice, and for the first time William saw how small and tired they looked.

"She'll be all right, you'll see," he said.

Amanda had joined them now. "What a night," she said to no one in particular.

It was nearly dawn; the moonlight had gone, so that suddenly it was darker than the night had been.

"There's a fog. I can feel it," Amanda said "Oh, God!"

"She will die of exposure," Helen stated, in a voice of doom.

"Not in September," replied William.

They could hardly see anything, though in the east there was a faint rosy glow shining through the darkness and fog.

"Morning will be here in a minute. Dawn is often like this," said William, trotting across stubble.

Suzy whinnied to Boxer, and he answered. Then

another pony whinnied and Mickey Mouse came cantering towards them, his reins wound round his hoofs, a stirrup missing. Alice jumped off and caught him, while Helen said, "She must have fallen off, then. She isn't just lost. What will Mum and Dad say? I wish we'd never come."

"We told you not to bring her, not once but several times," replied Amanda, sounding something like her mother.

Then Alice screamed, "Look at his knee. It's sticky, covered with blood."

William slid off Boxer and found his torch and, crouching on the ground, looked, while in the distance there was the mournful sound of another siren going off. It's like a war, he thought, nothing but disaster.

"They hit the wall," he said at last, standing up. "There's dust on his knee. You remember that wall? They must have tried to jump it. It's about half a mile back. Come on."

"He shouldn't trot, it's still bleeding," said Amanda, who wanted to be a vet. 'I'll stay with him. I've got a clean handkerchief. You go on. I'll follow slowly. I'll be all right."

"There was no way round," said Trudy.

"It must have been as high as Mickey Mouse's ears. It wasn't his fault. He must have tried. Poor Mickey Mouse!" said Alice.

They were stumbling over hillocks now. William slowed down. There were rabbit holes everywhere and a smell of thyme, and the grass seemed full of animals fleeing as they came.

"If she's dead, I'll kill myself, because it will be my fault, because I'm the eldest," Helen said.

"It won't help," replied William.

"But I shan't want to live," cried Helen, weeping.

William wished that Leon or Marvin had come too. They must be still at the farm watching the fires being put out, their eyes smarting with smoke, their faces black with it.

The rosy light had spread and deepened in the east and, suddenly, it was dawn. William could see the outline of the wall now and he was cold.

"Emily, where are you? It's us," called Trudy. "Emily! Emily!" And then, grey like a ghost, she was there, a small infuriated figure shouting at them.

"You left me, you beasts! You left me alone. And Mickey Mouse couldn't jump it. He tried and tried, and then he fell and you just went on. I hate you. You didn't care. He may be dead for all you care."

Her small face was twisted with fury. Her hat was covered with dust, her cheeks smudged with tears and dirt. William shone his torch on her and she yelled, "Put it off!"

"We've got Mickey Mouse, but he's hurt his knee. Amanda's leading him. We'll have to take it in turns to ride home," Helen said.

"We've been worried stiff, if you want to know," announced Alice.

They all dismounted, waiting for Amanda and the two ponies she was leading, to find a way round the wall. William didn't feel like talking; he felt flat, let down, and he had no energy left. They waited and ate the blackberries which grew near the wall, and called, "Amanda", and slowly the day grew lighter and the sky brighter.

We've failed, thought William, but only just. Tomorrow night the arsonist may strike again. We must split up more, carry whistles, and go without the Doyles. The air smelt of fire, the wind carried ashes on it.

"You've been very brave," Helen told Emily.

"No, I haven't. I cried and cried and one of my arms doesn't work, and I want Mummy. I want to be in bed at home. I wish I'd never come," shouted Emily.

They looked at her arm, but when they touched it she screamed, and Helen said, "I bet it's fractured.' And Amanda, approaching at last, called "A greenstick fracture."

They felt better with Amanda there. She was calm and sensible and soon had Emily on Suzy, while she rode Boxer and William walked, leading poor lame Mickey Mouse.

And so they limped back, making plans – the Doyles wondering what their parents would say, Emily's arm strapped to her side with a scarf, William saying, "We mustn't give up. I shall go out alone if none of you will come any more."

Amanda answered, "I shan't give up. Don't insult me please. I have never forgotten Tango disappearing. I never will. I shall go on searching for these awful people until they are caught."

And slowly, daylight came and the countryside came to life with it.

The Doyles' home was a slated Victorian house called 'Bide-a-Wee'. No one knew why it had such a name. Mr and Mrs Doyle were standing in the road waiting for them. Mrs Doyle wore horn-rimmed glasses and her hair was as tangled as their trees. Mr Doyle had broad shoulders and short legs, and hair which grew in all directions on his head.

"Oh, no! Oh, help!" cried Amanda. "They look furious. They'll kill us."

The Doyles began to cry and Emily called, "I've hurt my arm. I think it's broken."

William thought, give them time. Hold your horses, William, don't speak yet.

Amanda called, "She fell off. She shouldn't have come. We didn't ask her to."

"But you asked the others?" asked Mr Doyle, in a voice shaking with fury.

"Yes, I did, sir," replied William. "We are a Pony Patrol. We are looking for the man who burnt down our barns, and has now burnt down the Merriots'. We are on the side of law and order, sir. We are helping the police."

'Helping the police! Get out," shouted Mr Doyle. "Get out!"

"Go," said Helen. "Please go. We'll be all right."

"Yes, go . . ." urged Trudy. "Now, please. He'll kill you in a minute."

Mrs Doyle was carrying Emily into the house, which suddenly lit up as she slammed the front door shut.

"Will you be all right? He won't kill *you*?" William asked.

They shook their heads, dismounting, leading their ponies away past their father without saying a word.

"Don't ever come near here again. How dare you entice my daughters away?" shouted Mr Doyle.

"How dare you leave them alone at night, poor little devils," cried Amanda.

"The pony is hurt, too," said William suddenly remembering Mickey Mouse who Trudy was leading towards a dilapidated stable. "He needs a tetanus injection, perhaps stitching, a vet anyway sir, or he could die."

But Mr Doyle was shouting at them now.

"He's insane," said William, turning Boxer round. "We'd better go."

"Poor children," exclaimed Amanda, following. "What a father!"

"No wonder they're odd," said William.

"Will he beat them?" asked Amanda.

"I don't know. But they can't come again. They can't be in the Pony Patrol."

"No, never again," agreed Amanda.

"'Bide-a-Wee'," said William. "What a name for a house. Who would want to bide there?"

"He's mad," said Amanda.

'Supposing he's the arsonist?" asked William. "He could be. He's mad enough."

"But Mrs Doyle was with him, and Minnie."

"That's true." Suddenly the night seemed to have lasted for ever.

Milking had begun at Deep Wood Farm when they reached it. Everyone knew about the fire already.

"You weren't in time then?" asked William's father.

"You weren't quick enough then," said his mother.

"You had better move a bit faster another time,' said Pete.

"What happened then?"

"Where were you?"

"Didn't you see the blaze?"

He wanted to shout at them, but he didn't. And their questions went on, long after Amanda had gone, hammering away in William's brain. Where did we go wrong? he thought. How could we have been too late? Things must be organized better tonight. We can't fail again. We are going to be the laughing stock at Pullborough Market this Saturday, he thought, crawling into his pyjamas, lying down, worrying about the Doyles, imaginging headlines saying, "Girls whipped", imagining Mickey Mouse dying of tetanus while the arsonist burnt down barn after barn. We were too late, he thought. If we had been in time, we would be heroes now.

Three miles away, Natasha and Leon were listening to their father. He was a tall moustached figure trying to live in a world which didn't exist any more. Their mother was there too, beautiful in a rich coat.

"I approve of the Patrol," Mr Merriot was saying. "For once you are doing something concrete. Keep it up. Go out again tonight, take my binoculars. Ride fast, cover a large area. You lead, Leon, and make the decisions, boy. You have the background. Don't be led by a farmer's boy."

Amanda was at home too, now, eating her breakfast with her parents, saying, "We rode all night, but you don't mind, do you? You know William's all right. He's so sensible. It's really no more dangerous than cub hunting and you let me do that when I had Tango, didn't you?"

Marvin had returned earlier, putting Skinflint into his loose-box, before slipping upstairs and into bed while the rest of the house still slept. Now he was sleeping too, an exhausted dreamless sleep.

And the Doyles had been soundly scolded and put to bed, except for Emily who was travelling towards a hospital to be X-rayed, saying again and again, "It wasn't their fault, Mummy. Can't you understand? I made them take me. William didn't want me either. And what about Mickey Mouse? What about having the vet, Mummy?"

"Your new saddles have cost me a fortune. I'm not made of money," said Mrs Doyle, turning through the hospital gates. "And your father's furious."

Chapter Six

A fight

It was three o'clock in the afternoon when William woke up. His mother was standing over him holding a cup of tea, wearing her apron and old house slippers.

"It's getting late," she said. "And your Dad wants help with a cow that's calving."

"Late!" he said. "Not five o'clock yet?"

"No, three."

He gulped the tea quickly while he saw that the sun was streaming through the cracks in the curtains and heard the familiar sounds outside.

"The insurance man has been about the barns," his mother said. "Don't be long now."

The vet had come by the time William reached the yard, so he wasn't needed. The vet was a tall, good-natured man who said, "Pity about the barns. Have you got any more fodder yet?" William left his father to answer and went up the hill to catch Boxer and Suzy. The sun was in his eyes and he still felt half asleep. He gave them large feeds and brushed off yesterday's sweat, and all the time he was thinking about the night ahead – what it might bring, what disasters or triumphs.

Presently the calf was born and the vet was going. "Have you been to the Doyles – to 'Bide-a-Wee'?" called William.

"No, not today. What's wrong then?"

"Nothing much," said William.

It was then that he decided that nothing was going to go right from now on, and it was then that his mother chose to call, "William, there's a letter come for you. A lady in a car delivered it. She wouldn't stop. She was quite nasty when I asked her in."

It was a grubby letter addressed in a childish hand. William opened it with misgiving and read:

Dear William

We are never to see you again and you must never come near our house about anything at all. Emily has a broken arm. Mickey Mouse's leg is swollen and he may have to be put down and all because of you. Your name will be mud for ever in our house as long as we live. You are simply a horrible boy, and if Mickey Mouse dies we will blame you for ever.

Yours hatefully,

Alice, Trudy, Helen, Emily and Minnie Doyle.

It was written on a piece of lined paper and the ink was smudged in places. William read it twice, trying to take it in, to understand how feelings can change so quickly from friendship to hate. He felt numb, but then he had felt like that ever since the barns had gone.

"Is it important?" asked his mother, peering over his shoulder. "No, just silly. It's from the Doyles." He put the letter in his pocket and went back to the stables. I prefer horses to people, he thought, picking out Boxer's hoofs. If they like you, they like you for ever. They don't change their minds at the drop of a hat.

But now his mother was calling, "Telephone for you, William. I don't know who it is. Hurry now." And the cows were coming in to be milked, moving slowly deliberately across the yard.

"William here," he picked up the receiver.

"It's Leon. I've rung up about tonight," said the voice at the other end. "I want to lead the patrol tonight and I don't want the Doyles, they are no help at all."

"They aren't coming anyway," replied William.

"So there will only be the five of us then?" asked Leon.

"Yes, I think we should split up and carry whistles."

"But keep within calling distance, just spread out a bit. I've been looking at the map and I've got my father's binoculars," replied Leon.

"It may be dark or raining," replied William.

"And Natasha's bringing a camera. She wants to use it for evidence in case we see the arsonist, but don't catch him. And I'm thinking of bringing a gun," continued Leon.

"No. Not a gun. We must be like the police – unarmed," replied William.

"It's a revolver actually. I shan't use it unless necessary," replied Leon.

"When is necessary?"

"If he starts shooting at us, or if he's running away, I can shoot him in the legs. He deserves it. The damage he's done here is unbelievable. My father's giving me five hundred pounds if we catch him. Five hundred pounds! He wants him, dead or alive."

"You don't want to be tried for murder. You could shoot the wrong man in the wrong place. Have you thought of that?"

"I'm a crack shot. I'm in the Pony Club Tetrathlon team. See you tonight then, and I'm leading the patrol, right?" asked Leon.

"We'll see," replied William, putting down the receiver.

"Anything important?" asked his mother. "Not bad news?"

"No, nothing important," replied William.

It was six o'clock now and Amanda was arguing with her mother, who was making curtains.

"I tell you, I'm going. I'm not staying here. I've promised William. I'm doing a public service. I'm not going to a disco till midnight like my friends. I'm searching for the arsonist. Can't you understand?" wailed Amanda.

"You can't go out night after night. It isn't right," said her mother. "You could be murdered."

"Not with William," replied Amanda, putting on her riding coat. "Anyway, the Merriots are coming and their parents actually approve, so it must be all right."

"This must be the last time, then," said her mother with a mouth full of pins. "I shan't sleep a wink while you're out, nor will your father."

"I'm sorry, but I have to go, because I've promised," replied Amanda, looking for her riding boots. "Anyway, I'm a member of the patrol now, and that's binding."

"If only you liked sewing or something a bit

47

feminine," complained her mother. "Horses are all right when you are little, but you're a teenager now."

The telephone started to ring then. It was William. He said, "Bring a whistle if you've got one. There's lots of complications. I'll tell you when you come." He sounded miserable.

"I've only got one I had in the Girl Guides years ago."

"Bring that then," he said.

"If you get hurt I shall blame myself for ever," announced her mother.

"I shan't. I'm tough," said Amanda, touching wood.

William was eating two fried eggs, three sausages and a piece of fried bread, when Amanda arrived at the farm.

"Have you eaten?" he asked, looking tired and dishevelled, with lines round his eyes which hadn't been there before.

"Yes, thank you."

"Have a cup of tea, anyway," said his mother.

Amanda loved the farm kitchen with its old stone floor, its huge old-fashioned dresser hung with mugs and decorated with plates. It had an Aga and a large scrubbed table in the middle, and old-fashioned wooden kitchen chairs and an enamel sink and three comfortable chairs, and piles of unpaid bills mixed with schedules of long-forgotten horse shows on the mantelpiece. Cats snoozed comfortably on the chairs. The window ledges were covered with Mrs Gaze's plants in pots, and a pair of stirrups hung among coats on a row of hooks by the back door.

"Sit you down. Make yourself at home. Just push

off one of the cats," said Mrs Gaze.

I'm at home already, thought Amanda. Why isn't my home like this? Instead of everything being clean and tidy and the latest thing from London?

"Leon wants to lead the patrol. Do you think it's fair?" asked William, putting down his knife and fork.

"No. It was your idea. He can't pinch it. You thought up everything. I'll speak to him," said Amanda. "Don't worry, I'll put him straight."

"If he leads, I'll go by myself," said William. "He had the best of you with him last night. I just had the Doyles and just see what happened. He can't always have his own way. He wants to bring a gun too."

"Stupid fool."

"The Doyles aren't coming. I've had a letter," continued William. "They hate me. I'm never to go near them again – as if I want to!"

His mother was listening, raising her eyebrows and muttering under her breath. I'm a failure, William thought. Leon's right. I can't lead.

"We ought to take an oath, to write a constitution. We need rules," said Amanda. "As for the Doyles, I shouldn't bother. They aren't worth it."

He remembered the night before. He had liked the Doyles and he had thought they had liked him. He had done his best too, and now he had to take the blame for everything.

"We'd better tack up. Come on," said Amanda.

William took his dirty plate to the sink.

"Be careful, son," his mother said. "Look where you're going."

"I always do."

"Touch wood," said Amanda.

It was growing dark already and the sky was full of cloud. Outside the yard smelt of cows and burnt straw. In the distance tractors were going home along a lane.

William had a knife in his pocket, a whistle, a piece of string and some money. He tacked up Boxer in silence. Mounting, he suddenly wished he was going hunting, hacking – anything but on another night's excursion with Leon. He hadn't shown Amanda the Doyles' letter, because it hurt him too much even to think about it. Leon would not have cared; he would have turned the whole affair into a joke, but William felt differently.

There was no moonlight tonight, just the straight, twilit road to the pub, the horses' hoofbeats, the jingle of bits, and Amanda who was silent too, wondering what would happen when Leon and William met.

Leon and Natasha were waiting, Leon wearing an ancient hunting coat which had belonged to his grandfather, Natasha carrying a hunting whip.

Marvin was coming down the road, calling, "Mum knows. She's furious. I must be back by twelve, because Skinflint cost two thousand and we can't risk his knees. Mrs Doyle telephoned. It was awful."

Leon said something rude about Mrs Doyle. Natasha said, "Stupid old cow."

"This is all of us, then," said William. "We are not many tonight." He looked at Leon and felt the hair stand up on the back of his neck like the hackles on a dog's back.

"I'm taking over as leader. I'm going to get some new blood from somewhere," Leon announced.

Deep down, right from the beginning, William

had known there would be trouble between them, but it had come even sooner than expected.

"We have a military background, it's built into us to lead," Natasha said.

"But William started it. It was his idea," answered Amanda. "He's always been leader."

"Not now, not any more," replied Leon.

"Our family has been leaders for six hundred years," replied Natasha.

"I'm leading," said William, his voice suddenly obstinate, his jaw set. "I know the land, I know the farmers. They are my friends. We like each other. They hate the Merriots."

Boxer backed away. Amanda shouted, "Don't start a fight. Don't be silly."

But now the boys were facing each other. "Can't you stop them?" asked Marvin.

"I *am* leading," said Leon. "We can't split up tonight, so I am leading."

"Wrong again," replied William.

"I'll kill you."

"Just try."

Suddenly they were riding at each other, grabbing hold, pulling each other's arms.

Leon yelled, "Give me your whip, Natasha."

Amanda shouted, "No you don't."

William hit Leon across the jaw. Boxer shied away, Flaming Prince reared.

"Stop it," cried Amanda. "Please."

Natasha started hitting Boxer with her hunting whip. It left weals on his sides. He reared and plunged and the old lady leaned out of the pub window, crying, "I'll call the police."

"I'm leading," cried William, with blood on his face.

"I am," shouted Leon, drawing his gun and pointing it at William's head. "I was born to lead."

"No one was born to anything," replied William. "But I don't want to lead the patrol if you're in it. I would rather ride alone, or be dead. You're a traitor, a liar, useless." He wasn't frightened of the gun, just suddenly tired of Leon, tired of them all. He rode away without another word and found that Boxer wouldn't walk any more and he knew that it could take months to win his confidence back. Most likely he would refuse to go near the pub again and never forget the whipping. He thought, I hate the Merriots, and I hate the Doyles, and even Amanda has let me down. But I shall go on alone. I shall never give up. And he was furious to feel tears pricking behind his eyes, and a sick feeling of misery in his stomach. You can't fight a man with a gun, he thought. I wasn't a coward. I was just fed up and I didn't see the point of being shot, and he imagined his blood staining the gravel outside the pub, and his mother crying and his father identifying the body.

He leaned forward to pat Boxer's sweaty grey neck and he thought, perhaps I should start all over again, and find new members and have a proper constitution like Amanda says. He rode without seeing anything along a straight, dark road, with fields of beet and turnips on each side, wondering whether he had done the right thing, and what Leon was saying, and he thought over and over again, you can't fight someone with a gun, but it didn't help. I should have stayed and faced the gun, he thought. Dad would have stayed. What made me leave? I wasn't scared. They'll call me a coward now and gradually everyone will know. But he knew it wasn't that which had made him leave – it was a sort of disgust, it was a feeling that the fight should never have been, that it was pointless; and there was Boxer too – Boxer being whipped for nothing, and not understanding. And if one had to die, one should die for something noble, not in a petty scrap outside a pub over next to nothing. It was all those feelings mixed together which made him ride on along the road without looking back.

Chapter Seven

Hospital

Rain started to fall but he didn't notice it. He began to blame himself, to doubt himself, to call himself a coward. He started to dread tomorrow and the next day and the day after, and he had never felt that way before. Boxer went on walking, his steps quick and fearful, his ears pricked.

Once William thought he heard someone shouting behind him, but he didn't stop, didn't care. He was still riding away from a scene he had hated, riding away and trying to forget and knowing he couldn't. He didn't stop to look at the signposts and Boxer was still too nervous to suggest turning for home, for he was hurt too and didn't understand.

Once William saw a police car in the distance and, automatically, turned off the road and rode behind a hedge over turnips until it had passed.

There was plenty of night life: hedgehogs in ditches, rabbits grazing short grass, night birds flying. Sometimes even a plane. Somewhere a clock chimed twelve and later still one o'clock and then at last, William stopped and said, ''We'd better go home, Boxer." It was very dark. He could just make out the road and the outline of trees and the telephone wires stretching across the horizon. And he felt empty now, as though he was a shell with everything inside swept away.

He turned Boxer round and let the reins lie loose on his neck, and Boxer started to walk again as he had all evening, quickly and fearfully. "You know the way. Just go home," William said. And he thought, I ought to sing; singing always makes one feel better. He knew Boxer would take him home, because he had never let him down yet. He was the sort of horse who would give you his last ounce of strength, who would go until he dropped. And he was wise too, and as clever as a cat. He was the best horse William had ever ridden.

The sky was lightening a little now and it had stopped raining. And for the first time William wondered where Amanda was and where Leon had led them and what they had found. He felt shut out, like a young colt shut out of a herd.

He thought, I should get off and rest old Boxer's back, I must have ridden miles. But he didn't seem to have any strength left. And then suddenly he knew where he was – he was riding down the road towards "Bide-a-Wee", and he remembered that he was not supposed to go near the house ever again, and he tried to laugh. Soon he could see the chimney and the grey outline of the slate roof, then. Boxer stopped and snorted. It's only the ponies, thought William, he can smell them, and he pushed him on with his legs. They were on the corner now, by the red brick garden wall and William remembered that they had been here roughly twenty hours ago and wondered why it seemed like weeks instead of hours. Then he saw that there was a van parked at the side of the road with its headlights off. He heard someone say, "What's that, Jim? It sounded like hoofs. Get a move on." William's heart started to pound against his sides.

"There's a horse out there, I swear, a grey . . ."

"More like a ghost."

"How many more saddles are there?"

"Only a couple . . ."

William slid to the ground and tied Boxer to a post with a bit of string. His emptiness had gone. He felt clear-headed and afraid, but he knew what he had to do. He felt for his whistle and his knife.

"Shut the door!"

They were carrying the last of the saddles from the saddle room down the short drive to the van. William slid along the ground behind the bramble bushes to the van. He knew he hadn't much time. His knife was open. He slid up to the tyres, stuck it in and pulled and pulled again. The brambles tore at his head, stuck in his hat. He heard one of the men saying, "What's that? Leave the gates for Gawd's sake."

He felt sweat running down him, and he prayed, God make it puncture, and then he heard a hiss growing louder and louder and he rushed for another tyre and stuck his knife in again and wrenched. But now the men were running towards him, dragging at him, kicking, and he put his whistle to his lips and blew, while they kicked; and he went on blowing until his hat cracked and now they had reached his head and everything was spinning and he thought with anguish, "What

57

about Boxer?" before he passed out in a rush of leaping stars.

He came to in a bed. His mother was beside him and his father was standing by a window, looking out of place in Wellington boots.

"What about Boxer?" he said. "Where is he?"

"He came home," his mother said. "How do you feel, son?"

His father came across now and said, "They caught the men. They were after the saddles – all brand new too."

He thought, I'm not concussed, I can remember, with a rush of joy. And he said "What about Boxer?" again.

"Right as rain, all tucked up with bran mash. He's at Amanda's place. She insisted – thought we wouldn't look after him properly. She's nursing him night and day."

"What time is it?"

"Two o'clock."

His head was bandaged. He felt sore all over, as though he had been beaten.

"There were two of them. I hadn't got a chance . . ." he said.

"The police heard your whistle. It was an old police whistle. One your Uncle James had years ago when he was a policeman," said his father, laughing.

William saw now that he was in a ward with high white walls and lots of beds. It hurt him to turn his head, but he was able to see some of the other patients, who looked old and frail.

"I did some good, then?" he asked with a sudden feeling of hope. "Someone must be pleased."

"I should think so, considering what they did to you. You've been unconscious and then asleep for close on twelve hours," his mother said.

"These came this morning at twelve," said his father, holding up some flowers in cellophane.

His eyes were heavy lidded, swollen. He wondered if he had a black eye. He wondered what had happened to the others, where Amanda was, whether they intended to go out tonight without him.

"Don't you want to know who sent them?"

"When am I leaving? That's what I want to know," he replied.

"*From Mr and Mrs Doyle with grateful thanks*," read his mother with such triumph in her voice that he suspected that she had found the letter. But now a nurse was coming across the ward saying "That's enough. He must rest. Is there anything you want, William? A drink or something?" He drank some water and watched his parents leaving, waving to him as they left the ward, mouthing "We will be back tonight."

The nurse put a thermometer in his mouth, took his blood pressure. "You'll do," she said. "Now what about a wash?"

He had never been in hospital before.

"You took a proper beating, didn't you?" asked the nurse. "You're a real hero."

"I don't feel like one," he answered, remembering how he had ridden away from Leon.

"Did the men run?" he asked.

"I think so. They tried to change a wheel, then ran away when the police came. Now stop talking. It will be tea time in a minute," the nurse said.

After tea, Amanda came hurrying across the ward.

"I'm only to stay five minutes," she said. "Boxer's all right. He went home. Your father found him in the morning waiting by the back door. You were nowhere to be seen; then the hospital and the police phoned. And your Mum phoned me and I've got Boxer because I wanted to make sure he was all right."

"He is, isn't he?"

"Except for a few cuts and scratches."

"What happened to you?"

"I had a row with Leon; then I tried to follow you. I called and yelled, but you never answered and I didn't know which way you had gone and it was pitch dark and Suzy was terrified of every passing car, so in the end I went to your place and put her out in the field and then walked home and ran straight into my father," she said. She looked clean and tidy and wide awake. "He doesn't like me being out at two in the morning by myself, so there was a terrible row. Anyway, to cut a long story short, Leon phoned this morning and I told him about you and he's filled with remorse; so we all met at about twelve o'clock and drew up a rough constitution for The Pony Patrol. It's here – look. We're not going to do anything unless you approve, that's why I brought it." She had a scroll of paper in her hand, with writing in different colours. He took it and sat up. His eyes didn't work very well and for a moment he felt a bit dizzy, then he read:

THE CONSTITUTION OF THE PONY PATROL

A leader must be elected by a ballot of all members.
All members must vow to obey the orders of that leader without argument or mutiny.

At least four meetings should be held a year to discuss policy.
Any reward should be shared equally among all members.
The motto of the patrol should be: Fight to the very end. Do good wherever possible. Never give up. Members must swear to this when joining.

"But who is going to be leader?" asked William, putting it down.

"You, of course. That's already agreed," replied Amanda. "There's got to be other arrangements, too. I don't think we can ride all night, ever again, because our parents are getting difficult. But we can discuss that when you're better. I must go now, nurse is coming, but can I say you approve of the constitution?"

He said, "Yes, it's marvellous, just right. But do you really want me as leader after last night?"

She nodded, getting up, saying to a student nurse, "It's all right, I'm going."

"And thanks for having Boxer," he called after her.

William lay back on the pillows seeing the Patrol growing stronger, riding out twenty-strong; seeing himself going first. He was very tired now and everything seemed to be swimming in front of his eyes, but it didn't matter now that he knew Boxer was all right and that the Patrol was going on. He felt as though he had been through a long dark tunnel and come out on the other side, bruised, but triumphant.

He slept for a time and then his parents were there again and more flowers and a great box of chocolates and a newspaper reporter and a policeman. He had a cubicle put round his bed and

61

they came to talk to him in ones and twos. He made a short statement to the policeman and a longer one to the reporter, who wanted to know why he was out at that time of night riding alone.

Then his parents came again, saying, "The Doyles rang up to enquire after you, and so did the Merriots. You're quite a hero."

And he thought, life is like a see-saw. You're up one minute and down the next.

"You saved all their new tack and the bingo money," his father said.

"Bingo money?"

"Yes. They run a dance hall and bingo. That's why they're out such a lot," his mother told him. She had put on her best suit, and a hat.

"Were they out last night?" he asked.

"Yes, and the police kicked up a fuss because the girls were all alone. They've got to have a baby-sitter in future and a good thing too."

"Poor little mites," he said. He was tired again now and he wished that his parents would go away, and soon they did, slipping away as he fell asleep again to dream of the Patrol riding out on a bright moonlit night singing as they went, their bits and stirrups jingling, their heads held high.

He woke once and said, "It's a new beginning. A better beginning. Everything's going to be all right." And a nurse who was passing said, "Pardon?" and he replied, "Nothing, nothing at all," and went back to sleep.

Chapter Eight

Another fire

The house looked smaller and older when William left hospital two days later, and he seemed to be smelling everything for the first time. His mother had tidied his bedroom and put flowers on his chest of drawers. He felt as though he had been away for a long time. He smelt of antiseptic and he thought, if I was a horse I would roll over and over and get up and shake myself and feel better. There was a letter from the Doyles waiting for him. He read it, sipping tea in the kitchen. It said:

Dear William,

We are all sorry and grateful at the same time. Sorry because we were horrid to you and grateful because you saved our saddles. Emily is better, but Mickey Mouse's knee is the size of a football – it's gone septic because no one did anything in time and the vet is very angry. He's coming every day and Mickey Mouse is having penicillin. It's lucky he hasn't got tetanus too. We hope your head is better. Dad says we can join your patrol if it doesn't go out at night, but we don't think you'll want us any more.

Yours gratefully and sorrowfully,
Helen, Trudy, Alice, Emily and Minnie Doyle.

"You should thank them for the flowers," said his mother, looking over his shoulder. "Though they seem to change their minds about you as often as a broody hen turns her eggs."

"It's not them. It's their parents," William said.

Boxer was still with Amanda. William felt on edge, still between two worlds – hospital and home.

"We are having a meeting this afternoon, after Amanda and Marvin get back from school. The Merriots haven't started school yet. Have any more barns been burnt down?" he asked.

"No, the arsonist's lying low for the moment," his mother said.

Later, the others came. Amanda had written out the constitution again and added: *The patrol will always go unarmed.* Leon and Natasha looked uncomfortable and Leon wouldn't look William in the face. Marvin looked scrubbed clean and uncomplicated. They read through the constitution each in turn and then raised their right hands and said, "I swear by Almighty God to abide by the rules." It was a solemn occasion. We need a flag, thought William, a dark blue one with a horse on it.

"I think we should do other things as well as look for criminals," said Amanda. We should look for sick horses, for horses not being fed in winter and for children being battered by their parents."

Leon looked scornful. "Most children are battered indoors, out of sight," he said.

"But we can look through windows, and keep our ears open," replied William.

It was an uneasy meeting, as though a truce had been arranged which could be broken at any time. William served coffee and biscuits in the sitting room, where the sofa needed stuffing and the carpet had a hole in it.

"Tomorrow's Saturday," said Amanda. "What are we going to do?"

"I've thought about it," William answered. "I thought some of us could sit at Weeks's farm with our horses, out of sight. Dad knows Mr Weeks and he's very old and worried. He's got arthritis and can't move fast. We can sit upstairs which gives you a marvellous view right across the vale, past the railway line to the old windmill."

"You mean at night?" asked Marvin.

"Yes, all night. But we won't be on the roads and we can take it in turns to sleep. Dad's mentioned the idea to the old man and he's dead keen. He's been sitting up on his own for nearly a week now with a gun on his knee. Surely your parents won't object to that? It's all in a good cause."

"You mean get there before dark?" asked Natasha.

William nodded. "Then there's Ash Farm. It's empty but there's a great barn full of wheat straw just by the back door. We could move in there and camp, and there's stabling for the horses. What do you think?" He was seeing it all in his mind's eye already. He still felt bruised all over, but he was ready to battle again. "I think the arsonist strikes when there's a full moon," he added. "Or when there's moonlight anyway, and there must be a fine night soon."

He had thought a lot in hospital, discussed tactics with his father and discovered that he was behind him all the way.

"We've got a friend who wants to come. She's not much of a rider, but we can mount her on Jack. He hardly moves. It would make one more. She's fourteen," said Natasha.

"What's she called? And is she sensible? We don't want anyone who will scream," asked Marvin.

"Maggy. Maggy Schuman. She's sweet," said Natasha.

"We need plenty of people if we're going to occupy two houses," replied Amanda.

"That makes six of us," said William. "It's hardly enough but it will have to do. How shall we split up?"

"I'll try to find someone else. What about Saskia? She's in my set at school and very brave. She's American and she can ride. Can you find a mount for her, William?" asked Amanda.

"I'll try, and if I can't, she can come on a bike. We'll need Thermos flasks too, food, matches, torches, first-aid kit. We'll need haversacks or saddle bags to carry it all," he said.

"She's small. She can ride a pony," said Amanda, still talking about Saskia.

They drank more coffee and Marvin said, "We need another boy. I'll try to think of someone."

Amanda asked, "Who will go where?"

"I think I'd better go to Mr Weeks's farm, becuase I know him, at least for the first time," William said. "Who will come with me?" Marvin raised his arm, and then Amanda.

"What about me?" asked Natasha. "I don't want to be always with my brother. It gets a bit dull."

"We'd better draw lots," William said, his throat suddenly dry.

So they wrote down their names on scraps of paper and put them in a hat, leaving William's out. "This is for Mr Week's farm," said Amanda, and she drew out Natasha's name, and then Leon's and Marvin's. "So that is that," she said, with disappointment in her voice.

"You will have to take the other group to Ash Farm, because you're experienced," William said.

"But it's only Saskia, Maggy and me," answered Amanda.

"I'll go with you," offered Marvin. "I don't mind."

"That's settled then," said William, standing up.

"I'll bring a chess set to pass the time," said Leon.

"I don't play chess," replied William. "I haven't the patience."

"Draughts then."

Marvin and Amanda left together, making plans.

William decided to catch up Willow for Saskia. She had been his first pony and was twenty years old now, but she would carry Saskia as far as Ash Farm, and she was the quietest pony on earth. A load of straw arrived at that moment and then another, and another, and his father came out of the house and said, "Don't be long; we'll need you for unloading."

"How much did it cost?" asked William.

"There's twenty tons and it cost thirty pounds a ton. Work it out yourself," his father said. "The animals have to eat; and there may not be any left anywhere by Christmas."

His father was always prepared for anything because he always expected the worst to happen. He was always too early for every train he had to catch, or appointment he had to keep. Punctuality to him was a sort of religion.

It can't be costing all that, thought William, walking up the hill towards Willow. It's far too much. Last year you couldn't give straw away.

He caught Willow and took her down to the stable. She nudged his pockets and rubbed her nose on his sleeve. She was glad to be used again. He checked her shoes and fetched her oats. He remembered winning a cup on her when he was nine years old for Minimus jumping – it was his first cup. He had lived for nothing but horse shows then; it had been like a madness. Nothing else mattered by comparison. After that it had been hunter trials, and now he cared mostly for hunting.

His mother came out to the stable to tell him not to move the straw. "You're not fit to lift bales," she said. "You're just out of hospital. I don't know what your father's thinking of. You're supposed to be taking it easy. You look tired to death already."

She was right of course, he was tired now, too tired almost to move, or speak, or think. His whole body was crying out for sleep. He went indoors and lay down on the sofa in the sitting room. His mother put a rug over him and he thought, there's still tonight. I must be fit for tonight, and then he slept and when he awoke Amanda was there, saying, "Your mother phoned me. I've tacked up the horses. I found a little saddle and a snaffle for Willow, and here's Saskia.

Saskia was small with dark hair cut urchin-style. "Willow looks real cute. I know I'm going to love her," she said.

"Do your parents know about tonight?" asked William, sitting up.

"She's staying with me," Amanda said.

"I would rather they knew."

It was dusk already. Is there going to be a moon? wondered William, running upstairs to fetch a coat.

"You haven't had your supper," called his mother.

"I don't want any," he said.

He could feel excitement burning inside him now like a fire just lit and growing stronger every minute. Amanda was making coffee for him in the kitchen. She was at home there, accepted by the family. No one bothered to put on airs for her, or to put the kitchen straight in her honour, as they did for some people.

Ten minutes later, they were mounting, old Boxer pawing the ground with impatience. Amanda had washed his tail, oiled his hoofs, groomed him until he looked fit for the show ring.

"I've loved having him," she said. "But he was getting lonely."

Willow looked small and old and happy. Suzy pranced and danced and tossed her head.

William pulled up Willow's girths. "Has she any vices?" asked Saskia.

"None at all." It was the truth. Willow had never put a foot wrong in any direction in her life. She was a perfect first pony.

"Give old Weeks my regards," called William's father. "Tell him he can sleep tight tonight."

"Right you are." William was mounted now. He pushed Boxer with his legs and knew how stiff he was still from the beating he had taken.

His mother leaned out of a window to call "Good luck". And he saw that the sun was going down above the trees on the hill like a great ball of fire.

"Back to the old pub," he said. "Come on."

They made a fine clatter along the road and Suzy pranced and shied, while Boxer got into his easy, steady stride which could go on for ever.

"I told Saskia's parents we were sort of camping out. They didn't mind," Amanda said.

"There's a telephone there. Ring us if anything happens. We'll do the same. I haven't written down the numbers, we'll have to look them up. Okay?"

"Okay."

They were at the pub now and Leon, Natasha and Maggy were waiting already.

"You're with us, Maggy," Amanda said. Jack was thin and old and not quite sound. His shoes clinked behind and they didn't fit in front. Maggy was a pale, fair child who lived with her widowed mother. William wondered why she had come.

"To Mr Weeks's farm then," said Leon. "I'll beat you there."

"I'm not racing," replied William. "I want to save Boxer from unnecessary wear and tear."

He was sorry to leave Amanda and Marvin. He didn't feel safe with Natasha and Leon. They weren't his kind of people, not even friends. He didn't trust them, not deep down inside himself.

It was three kilometres to the farm. Mr Weeks was waiting for them, when they reached it. "I've put hay in the stable for the horses," he said, hobbling after them on two sticks. Two collie dogs followed at his heels. "You can sleep tight tonight," William said. "We'll take it in turns to watch. You'll be all right, I swear."

"You did pretty well the other night, William," said Mr Weeks. "Your mum must be proud of you."

They put their horses away and climbed some

twisty, back stairs to a room which gave them a view for miles. "You'll have to keep the light off or he'll suspect something," the old man said. "Would you like some tea? I can make you a pot if you like."

"No, we're fine, thanks," replied William. "You have a rest."

"Old fool," said Leon, when he had gone. "Why doesn't he give up, let someone else have the land to farm? He can hardly walk. Why doesn't he go into an old people's home?"

"Because he doesn't want to," William replied.

"He should be made to, then. He can't farm properly like that."

"He manages."

"This house could be done up. It could fetch a fortune," Leon said. "What does the old man want with a house this size?" He was pacing up and down the room now, staring out of the window. "There's going to be a moon, and our friend likes a moon," he said.

"I'm scared," said Natasha. "I don't know why. I'm not usually. It must be the atmosphere."

William felt the same, but he knew it wasn't the atmosphere which scared him, but Leon.

The moon was new and rode high in the sky. Everything was very still and beautiful outside. The moonlight made the building look new, hid the cracks and missing tiles, made a sort of magic.

Leon bit his nails. "I'll take the first watch," he said. "What's the time?"

"Ten o'clock," replied Natasha.

"I'll take the next watch. Wake me at twelve," said William.

"I'm afraid to sleep," said Natasha. "I'm certain there's rats."

71

"I'll kill them if they come out," said Leon. "I'll enjoy stamping on them."

Mr Weeks had put mattresses and blankets out for them. William lay down. Leon stood staring out of the window, tall and fair-haired. I don't trust either of them, William thought, they aren't my kind. They're ruthless. I wish I had gone with the others . . . He was afraid to sleep but it came in the end, full of uneasy dreams, of footsteps on stairs and the crackle of fire, of Boxer dead, and a house burning, and then suddenly he heard Natasha calling, "The barn's on fire, William. Wake up." And reality came back and suddenly he was alone running down the stairs, out into the night. Mr Weeks was there before him, beating at the fire with a stick. Natasha had a bucket of water. Leon had a hose and was connecting it to a tap. "It's all right. We're in time," said Mr Weeks, turning to William. "I don't know why you didn't see it though. Lucky I sat up, wasn't it? My old dog heard it first. He knew there was someone out there. You can always trust a dog. He may be old, but his hearing's all right."

Hens were cackling in a hen house. A bird swooped screaming in the sky. It wasn't dawn yet. William looked around him.

"Did anyone see anything?" he asked. "What about you, Leon?"

"I saw the fire. I was still on watch. I should have woken you, but you looked so comfortable and I knew I wouldn't sleep. I heard the dog barking and saw the fire. I screamed at Natasha and ran . . ."

Suddenly it was like playing "Murders" again at home, when William was small. The same sort of questions, the same sort of answers; the only difference was that this was in earnest. William started to look for footprints. He was overcome by a sense of failure. He had told Mr Weeks to sleep, that everything would be all right and then let the old dog raise the alarm. The fire was really out now.

"He won't come again now," said Mr Weeks. "You may as well go home. But I hear you've got some more straw in, William, so that will need some watching too."

It wasn't even dawn yet, but the moonlight was fading. Home! Home was a place you went to like a lair when you were tired or hunted. Suddenly, William felt both.

"The old dog didn't smell anything. The fire must have been a long time smouldering. It gave the arsonist time to get away and save his skin," continued Mr Weeks. "Good thing I kept my clothes on, though, wasn't it?" He gave a cackling laugh and went hobbling into the house on his two sticks.

"What's the time?" William asked.

"Two o'clock."

They all felt cold suddenly. "I shall go to Ash Farm first," William said.

"We'll go straight home," said Leon.

They led their horses out and tacked them up.

"Cheer up. The straw and hay are saved, even if we didn't do it all on our own," said Natasha.

"You mustn't seek glory," said Leon. "And as the old man said, you'd better watch your own."

"I'm not seeking anything. I just wish I had been awake as arranged and Mr Weeks hadn't got there first. If you want to know, I feel a failure!" yelled William, turning Boxer's head towards Ash Farm, with rage in his heart.

Chapter Nine

Catch the blighter

When William rode into the yard at Ash Farm, Marvin was keeping watch. He opened the back door a crack and said, "The girls are asleep upstairs. What's happened? Why are you here?"

Dawn was just breaking. In the distance, cocks were crowing.

"We've had our fire. We may as well go home," William said. He told Marvin what had happened. "And you never saw the arsonist at all?" asked Marvin.

William shook his head. "No one did." He had a suspicion now at the back of his mind, something he wouldn't even accept himself but which stayed just the same.

"It's certainly odd," said Marvin. "Surely Leon should have seen somebody in the yard? Fires don't just start themselves."

"A man could have crept round behind the barn and thrown a lighted match and then run to a car parked on the road. It could have been done in less than five minutes," William answered. "That must have been how it happened."

"But there was a moon," argued Marvin. "Leon

would have seen him running down the drive."

"Perhaps he was asleep. Perhaps he was woken by the dog, like old Mr Weeks," replied William wearily. "I just wish he had woken me, because it was my turn to watch."

"I don't like any of it. I don't like Leon. If his barn hadn't been burnt down I should say he wasn't on our side," Marvin said.

"I know he isn't on mine," replied William.

"Exactly. That's why he didn't wake you up. He wanted to pretend that you'd slept through your watch."

"We can't have suspicion among us. We've got to trust one another," said William.

"The Merriots are an odd lot, everybody knows that," answered Marvin.

"Let's go home, anyway," suggested William. "The night is past and there isn't a moon any more. He won't strike again."

They rode home mostly in silence. They went the long way round, past the Merriots' house so that Maggy stayed with them. Jack was tired and his shoes grew looser. They were all depressed by William's story.

"I'm all right now," said Maggy, when they reached the wrought-iron entrance gates to the house. "I'll go round the back to the stables. We live above them. Mum looks after the horses. Thank you for coming with me."

"Thank you for coming," replied William.

Saskia seemed half asleep. William dropped her, with Amanda, at Amanda's house in spite of their protests and then rode home alone with his two ponies and Boxer. But felt strangely happy now, probably because he trusted his ponies and they trusted him, so that they went well together with their ears pricked. It's Sunday, remembered William. Next week the Merriots go back to school and we haven't caught the arsonist, yet. Time is running out.

William watered his ponies, fed them and turned them out. His mother had breakfast waiting for him in the oven. His father had been up most of the night with a calving cow. William felt as though time had suddenly accelerated; his life seemed to be hurtling past at seventy miles an hour instead of the usual thirty. Too much had happened in too short a time. He would have liked a rest but tomorrow there was school, full of dreary lessons, maths he could never understand, science which he loathed. He felt drained of energy and knew he had yet to recover from the shock of being kicked. He didn't feel ready for the school, for the petty, mean teasing, for the girls who followed him mockingly and for his enemies among the boys.

"Sit you down. Have a rest. You look all in," his mother said. She always knew how he felt. He started to tell her about the night; then his father called, "Willow's got the colic, William. Come here, will you? She's pretty bad." And he thought, not something else, not poor little Willow. She was in the stable trying to lie down. "Hang on while I get a drench," his father said.

She was soaked in sweat. William walked her round and round the box, shouting, "Stand up, will you? Keep going," automatically, while his heart seemed to be sinking lower and lower into his boots. He held her tongue, which was moist and strong, while his father poured down the drench which smelt of turpentine. It ran down their arms and dripped on to the straw.

"We'll see what that does for her," his father said.

"I think we need the vet," replied William.

"We'll give her another twenty minutes or so. Keep her moving . . ."

Willow hung her head now, her eyes were half closed. She was waiting for the pain to come back.

"It's spasmodic," William said.

"Did you bring her back warm?"

William shook his head. "We walked all the way."

"Where did she spend the night?"

"In the barn at Ash Farm."

"Did she have anything to eat?"

"I don't know." William had the feeling it had all taken place before. That he had stood like this with his father long ago with a sick pony between them. They were both tired out. And now Willow was trying to roll again. "She's not any better, please get the vet," he pleaded. "She's probably got a chill after last night. Suzy's all right, isn't she? So there can't have been anything poisonous in the barn."

He led her outside to where the sun was shining. He talked to her, saying, "You'll be all right soon, I promise. Steady, little pony. Steady." He blamed himself for lending her to Saskia, for giving her oats when she was not used to them.

The cows had been milked and were going out to pasture. Willow was sweating. The drench hadn't worked. She threw herself down and William had to hit her to get her up again. He felt sick suddenly, sick of everything. "He's coming," said his father, returning. "He won't be long. She'll be all right now. What happened last night?"

William told him and he said, "You should have phoned the police. They might have found a clue. Always phone the police." His father always knew what should be done. William envied him for it and for his lack of doubt about anything.

Ten minutes later a new vet came and asked questions and gave Willow an enema, and the sun went in again and they could hear the church bells calling worshippers to Matins. The new vet was a pale young man with long fingered hands and fine features. He injected Willow with sedatives and asked more questions. William's mother brought them tea in mugs and they stood and watched Willow and, gradually, the pain went out of her eyes and she grew sleepy, and they felt better.

"She's a grand pony," said William's father. "We wouldn't want to lose her, would we, William?"

"She taught him to ride," his mother added.

Presently the young vet went away, saying, "Call me if you have any more trouble. The sedative will wear off in a few hours. Keep an eye on her, won't you?"

"That's that, then," said his father. "More money gone west."

William put Willow in a loose-box and tried to watch her for another hour, but most of the time he slept, while she stood drugged and quiet, watching him. Then he heard his mother calling him in to lunch. He felt Willow's ears before he went inside, and she nuzzled his pockets, and he said, "You'll be all right now."

There was roast beef and three veg and Yorkshire pudding, followed by suet pudding. None of them felt like talking. Finally, William's father said, "Funny old Weeks should spot the fire first last night, because he's hard of hearing. I can't make it out."

And his mother said, "He can hear what he wants all right."

William ate too much and felt weighed down afterwards. He returned to Willow's box and found her lying down. He sat beside her until his mother called, "Telephone. Hurry. It's Amanda."

He ran indoors then, thinking, what now? Dreading bad news, he picked up the receiver and she said, "Hullo. What about tonight? The Merriots go back to school tomorrow and it's going to be a fine night. I've just heard the weather forecast. It's our last chance."

"For what?" he asked, to gain time.

"To catch the arsonist. Natasha's just phoned and she wants just the five of us to go to Ash Farm, and to have a sort of party at the same time as watching. They're going to bring shandy or something. What do you think?"

"You mean us and Marvin and them?"

"That's right. They won't be back again till half-term and goodness knows when that will be," Amanda answered.

"As long as we don't take shifts. I don't want to miss anything tonight," he said.

"They're lending me Jack," she said. "We'll meet there. Okay?"

"Okay." He put down the receiver slowly. He was filled with a feeling of panic. He felt as though he was about to ride into some sort of trap. But what trap? He thought, me and Marvin. She doesn't even need Suzy. She's joining them, and it frightened him.

He went back to Willow. She was still lying

80

down, but she looked peaceful and wasn't in any pain.

He went up the hill to look at the other horses. They whinnied to him, and stood around him in a group, while he stood staring down on the flat field criss-crossed by dykes, and he thought, I shall be glad when tonight is over. The night seemed to be waiting for him like a river to be crossed or a fence to be jumped, huge and formidable, with danger lurking at every turn.

His mother didn't want him to go. "You're tired," she complained. "Just look at yourself in the mirror. There are dark circles under your eyes. You look terrible, William, and you're back at school tomorrow. You can't go on like this."

"It's the last time," he replied. "There's going to be a moon. We must try once more."

"If only you had something to go on, some lead. You don't even know what he looks like," complained his mother. "And you've taken one beating. Isn't that enough?"

"It's the last time," he repeated. "After tonight, I'm concentrating on school." He put on a big pullover, his stretch jodhpurs and his rubber riding boots. He hadn't had time to buy a new hat; it lay shattered somewhere, or the police had it, he didn't know and didn't care.

"You'll be going to court soon, too, to give evidence," his mother said. "And that will mean missing school, and you can't keep missing school."

"I know." It worried him too, but he wouldn't admit it. He caught Boxer and fed him. He looked at Willow who was feeling more lively now and had drunk a bucket of water and was munching hay.

He wandered outside and looked at the new

81

straw stacked under a tarpaulin. He felt restless. He wanted time to pass, the night to be over, but now, suddenly, time seemed to be standing still. He thought of Amanda with the Merriots, saw her mounting poor decrepit Jack, laughing, riding towards Ash Farm with them and, at that moment, he didn't seem to have a friend in the world. Dusk was coming now. Another day was nearly gone. It had been a very long day.

His mother came out to see him off, saying, "Be careful, son. What about your hat? Couldn't you borrow one?"

"I'll try," he said, to please her.

The moon was up already, vying with the sun which was sinking in the west. There was a bite in the air and a cow was calling to her calf.

He said, "See you in the morning, Mum."

She looked small and worried, watching him ride away and he thought, this is how sons went to the wars long ago. She called, "Don't be late, and stay with the others. Don't take on anyone alone, please, William."

He smiled and waved and pushed Boxer into a trot and saw his father coming home from the fields on a tractor.

"You catch him tonight," his father shouted. "Don't you sleep through anything – you catch the blighter." He sat broad-shouldered and red-faced on the tractor, an old hat on the back of his head – part of the landscape.

"I'll do my best," William answered.

The road was straight and empty and, presently, he was riding down the lane to Ash Farm, singing old war songs to give him courage, songs his father sang.

Chapter Ten

Remember Waterloo

They were there before him. William tied up Boxer in the barn. The electricity had been cut off and it was nearly dark now. He found the Merriots, Amanda and Marvin sitting upstairs playing cards by the light of a lantern.

"You've made it, then," Leon said.

The farmhouse had lots of small rooms, two staircases and two kitchens, because once it had been two cottages. It was very old and the brick floors downstairs dipped in places, worn down by the tread of years of boots. It smelt damp and the wallpaper was coming off the walls. The windows were small and looked across silent, empty fields. There was no other house nearby.

"We're playing poker," Leon said.

"I'll watch for the arsonist then," replied William, going to the window. "What does he look like? Does anyone know?"

"Small and cunning like a rat," Amanda answered.

"Thin like a diseased cat," said Marvin.

"Mad with sacks round his shoulders," answered Natasha.

"Tall and dashing, like a highwayman," suggested Leon, dealing cards.

"I'll look for all of them, then," exclaimed William. He felt like his father, as though he alone belonged here. He knew the land, he knew the feel of the earth, the way sugar beet grew, the size of a good turnip. He knew why a cow was lowing, and whether a tractor was pulling properly on all its cylinders. He knew the sort of people who had lived in Ash Farm in the past – small, humble people who worked from dawn to dusk. People who had asked for very little from life. He was the only one who really belonged in the house – the others were alien – they belonged to mansions, to apartments, to single rooms in large houses. But his forebears had raised families in such a house.

Outside nothing seemed to move. The sun had gone. The moon rode proud and alone in the sky. He thought about Willow. Had the sedative worn off yet? Supposing it had, and she had another spasm? He should have asked his parents to look at her, just once more, before going to bed. The others were throwing down their cards now. Leon had won again. William suspected him of cheating because he always had the winning hand. He watched cars moving along distant roads. How did the arsonist travel? he wondered. By car, bicycle, motor bike? Or on foot, creeping like Guy Fawkes, with matches and paraffin in his pocket instead of gunpowder? What made him destroy so much beautiful hay and straw? Who did he hate? Animals, or humans?

"Are you going to play now?" It was Amanda speaking.

William shook his head. "I don't play cards," he

said. It wasn't true. He played sometimes at home on long, dark evenings. He simply wasn't in the mood now. He wanted to stand at the window staring out at the land he loved. The earth was full of shadows. A huge heap of sugar beet looked menacing in the moonlight, like a monster.

"Why won't he play?" demanded Leon. "I wanted to win some money off him."

"I haven't any money." It was true. He had forgotten to put any in his pocket. He hadn't even enough for a telephone call.

"You can owe it to me," Leon said.

"I don't play cards." A cat was walking along a hedgerow, creeping like a miniature tiger, its eyes two small green headlights in the dark.

"Are you going to stay in front of the window all night then?" asked Leon.

"Yes, that's what I came for."

"Have a drink anyway," suggested Amanda. They were opening bottles now, pouring drinks into glasses. He felt outside them, as though he didn't belong.

"It's meant to be a party. Don't be a spoilsport. What are you sulking about, anyway?" Marvin asked.

'I came to catch the arsonist."

"So have we. But we might as well have a bit of fun as well," said Natasha.

"Remember Waterloo," William replied.

"What about it?" asked Leon.

"They were dancing and having a party when they were attacked."

"But they still won. I know, because my great-great-uncle was there commanding his regiment," Leon said.

"Great-great-great-uncle." Natasha corrected him.

"What was *your* great-great-great-uncle doing then? Turning clods, I suppose," Leon said. "Your're just a farmer's boy, William. You haven't any blue blood in *your* veins."

"Shut up," cried Natasha. "Have a drink, come on, William." She put an arm round his shoulder, pushed a lemon shandy under his nose. "Don't listen to him. Just have a drink," she said.

He wished he was alone. He could see cars still going along a road, though it must be midnight now. He drank the shandy and thought, I wish I hadn't come. I could have gone somewhere else by myself. The others were talking about him now, and he had never felt so completely alone before.

"He's scared of playing," Leon said, in a voice loud enough for him to hear. "He's a wimp. If he wasn't he would hit me now."

"Shut up," said Amanda. "He's the bravest of us. Look how he took on those men with the van empty-handed."

"I would have done the same," retorted Leon.

"Would you?"

"Of course, and come off better."

"I hate this," Marvin exclaimed. "It's so petty. Let's have another game."

They played on, while William decided that he shouldn't lead the Patrol any more, since he didn't really belong. Leon had been right all the time. He was a born leader. He fitted in. His image was right – whatever that meant. The moon was higher in the sky now, indescribably beautiful. She dappled everything with silver. And the hours were passing; one knew now, without knowing how, that another day would soon begin. William could not believe that in seven hours he would be at school, that the night would be gone and the Patrol would cease to exist, at least for a time.

He wondered what lies the others had told their parents about tonight.

"My turn now at the window," said Leon, suddenly, behind him. "Come on, you're not the only hero here."

"You're welcome," replied William. "But there's nothing to see."

"I can still watch."

William sat down with Amanda. Suddenly they were all on edge, Leon most of all, standing at the window biting his nails, saying, "There's certainly a moon tonight."

The room was too small to contain all their emotions. Natasha was so tall her head nearly touched the ceiling. Marvin looked cramped sitting on the floor and now Leon blocked out all the moonlight coming through the window.

"Pass me another drink," said Leon. "Come on, don't argue." Amanda passed him a can of beer and, for a moment, moonlight flooded the room, while he drank.

"It's three o'clock," said Marvin, consulting his watch.

"Three more hours to go," exclaimed William. "I hope the horses are all right." He started to tell them about Willow. "I may have to go home soon to see how she is," he said. "I forgot to tell my parents to check on her last thing."

"Poor Willow. Was it our fault?" asked Amanda.

"More likely mine. I kept stuffing her with oats," replied William.

"My God, this room is oppressive," cried Leon. "If only the window was bigger. It lets in hardly any air. I feel as though I'm stifling."

"I'm sure there are rats in the thatch," said Natasha, who had an allergy to rats. "I heard a squeak just now."

"There's only a few more hours to go," replied William.

"I shall have to go outside," said Leon, lighting a cigarette. "You don't mind, do you? I won't make any noise. I'll just check on the horses and take a walk and come back."

Marvin took over at the window. They heard Leon's feet clattering down the uncarpeted twisty stairs.

"He never can stay anywhere long. He gets claustrophobia or something." Natasha explained. "Dad's the same. He can't go on an escalator if there are other people on it. It drives him mad."

"It's not long now, soon be dawn," said William, more to himself than anyone else. He felt very tired; standing by the window had kept him awake. Now, siting down on the hard dusty floor, he couldn't stay awake a moment longer. He slumped forward and dreamed that Willow was dying. She had twisted a gut and no one could save her. He woke with tears running down his face. Amanda was standing by the window now, and in the distance the first cocks were beginning to crow.

"I must see Willow," cried William, standing up. "I'm sure she's ill again."

Leon was still missing and outside the moonlight was beginning to fade. "It's like the ten green bottles," complained Natasha. "Now there are only three of us."

"It hasn't been much of a party, and I feel sick," said Amanda.

"I can't help worrying about Willow. She was my first pony," William answered.

Marvin started to drink again. He wasn't used to alcohol and he felt strangely elated. He started to sing *Why are we waiting*, slurring his words together, as William bent his head and went down the twisty stairs into what had once been a living room, and then out into the early hours of the morning. It was a raw morning, a beginning of winter. Boxer was standing in the barn with his head hanging. He whinnied when he saw William, glad to be released at last.

William tacked him up. He couldn't see much but found everything by touch, imagining himself a blind man.

"We are going home to see poor Willow," he told Boxer. "And then, if she's all right, I'll get a few hours' sleep before school. Mum will be pleased, at any rate . . ."

He could hear Marvin still singing as he rode across the yard and on to the road. I hope he gets home all right, he thought, remembering his very refined parents who kept such a tidy house and kept Skinflint wrapped in bandages like an old-fashioned baby in binders. He couldn't see much, but Boxer knew the way.

"I wouldn't change you for any of their horses," William said, riding on a loose rein. "You've got more sense than all their well-bred animals put together." Then his thoughts went back to Leon and he realized that Flaming Prince hadn't been in the barn when he fetched Boxer. Checked Princess had been restless without him, neighing and pawing the ground; it had hardly registered with him at the time but now it hit him like a sledge-hammer. I'm the leader, he thought, and Leon shouldn't have gone without any permission. Where is he? Why did he go? We'll have to expel him from the Patrol. He isn't any good if he hasn't the patience to wait and watch. And he smokes all the time, which is dangerous. He was trotting now witout realizing it, worrying, without really knowing what he worried about.

Gradually the trot became a canter, and for a moment the moonlight brightened and he could see the landscape lying before him like some exquisite picture. I've seen so many dawns, he thought, dawns waiting for cows to calf, dawns with sick animals, winter dawns when the milking has to be done and Pete's away.

He could see Deep Wood Farm lying before him now, set out like a model farm, with the house in the middle and the trees behind it touched with silver in the moonlight.

"We'd better slow up. We don't want you to return home hot," he said, making Boxer walk.

He could see the straw now, stacked where the Dutch barn had stood, covered with a shiny waterproof sheet. It didn't look much to feed a herd all through the winter.

Boxer wouldn't walk. He wanted to be home, for he loved the farm. His ears were wet with sweat and he kept going sideways and tossing his head. And William kept saying, "Steady, steady," and worrying about the straw and what there would be left for the animals to eat after Christmas. His father thought fodder would go down in price, that hay might be as little as £60 a ton again by January.

But supposing it didn't go down? What then? he wondered.

He stopped to look at a bicycle flung down at the side of the road, its owner nowhere to be seen. He got off and searched through the saddlebag and found only an old rag inside, and a couple of spanners. It had a flat tyre and no pump. He re-mounted and rode on. He was nearly home now. He decided he would have a hot drink before he went to bed, a huge mug of hot chocolate and some biscuits.

He was trotting again now, without realizing it, because he wanted to get home, and then he saw something which made him stop in his tracks, which set his heart pounding against his ribs, and he yelled, "Oh no! Not again!"

The next second he was galloping, yelling, "Fire! Fire! The straw's on fire." Reliving the time before when the barns had burnt down, with a mixture of fear and rage and indescribable horror. Boxer's hoofs sent sparks flying on the stoney drive to the farm, while William screamed "Fire! Fire! Fire! Get the police!" until he felt his lungs would burst, and then at last, as he reached the yard, a window opened in the house and he heard his mother call, "What is it?" And he yelled, "The straw's on fire." And he thought, why weren't we here instead of at Ash Farm? Why did I ever leave here? Why isn't Dad sitting up with a gun on his knee? Why are we such fools?

And then he saw something which made his blood turn cold and, for a moment, he stopped in disbelief and stared and thought, it can't be true!

And then without thought, automatically, he was galloping again, yelling. "You swine! I'll kill you! You filthy swine!" He was shouting words he didn't know he knew, galloping out of the yard as the arsonist fled, crouched low over a horse's neck.

Chapter Eleven

Why did you do it?

Amanda was clearing up. Marvin felt sick and sat doubled up in a corner. Natasha wanted to leave everything as it was, with the beer and shandy cans lying everywhere, and match-ends and cigarette-ends on the floor.

"After all, we won't be coming again," she said. "So why bother?"

"It isn't our place. We can't leave it like this. It spoils the reputation of the Patrol," Amanda answered, knowing that she sounded like a school Teacher or a prefect. "Anyway, it's illegal to leave things lying about."

"Not inside, outside, you fool," insisted Natasha. "I wonder where Leon is. He's a bit of a problem these days. He failed all his exams, and I passed mine and I'm younger. It just doesn't make for a happy family atmoshpere. And Dad's furious. Leon's cost thousands of pounds in education and now he's failed the lot."

"Poor Leon!" Amanda was wishing now that she had come here with William. She didn't know why she had chosen to go with the Merriots. It had been a mad decision, and she hated riding Jack.

Marvin was staggering about now, saying, "I want to go home."

"Don't worry, we are just going," replied Natasha. "We're just waiting for Amanda to finish the housework."

And I was looking forward to this day, thought Amanda. I thought we were going to have a super party and end up friends, real friends, all of us. But now I'm left with these two – ghastly, stuck-up Natasha who talks so posh she makes you feel sick, and Marvin who *is* sick.

Dawn was breaking as they went outside. They stood and looked across the fields and, suddenly, Amanda cried, "Look! Look over there! Fire!"

The horizon was lit up with leaping flames, far brighter than the rising dawn.

"It's Deep Wood. That's where it is," screamed Amanda. "It's William's farm. Come on, tack up. Get cracking. Poor William!"

She knew she would be left behind. Skinflint was fast. Checked Princess was thoroughbred. Suzy could have kept up with them, but not Jack. She felt like crying.

"Open your mouth, you fool," she shouted, trying to force the bit between Jack's ancient teeth.

"I can't wait," yelled Natasha, leaping into her saddle. "It's too awful for waiting," and she was gone in a rush of flying gravel.

"I shan't wait either," yelled Marvin, vaulting on to Skinflint, forgetting for the first time in his life how much he was worth, disappearing flat out, his hoofs pounding the road, sending up sparks behind them.

William was still chasing Leon.

"Why? Why?" he was asking himself. "Why has he done it to us? Is this the first time, or did he start all the others? Even his own fire?"

Flaming Prince was thoroughbred and faster than the wind, but William knew how to cut corners, how to keep up with faster horses, how to win against the clock in the show ring, and win on speed hunter trialling. And daylight was coming and he knew the countryside. He rode with his head, looking ahead, judging the lie of the land, avoiding the plough. Leon rode like a devil without thought or speech. He rode straight as a die, over dykes and streams, over a five-barred gate. And Flaming Prince sensed his desperation and didn't stop, but with the blood of his ancestors in his veins, he raced to win. In a matter of seconds he was unstoppable, a horse obsessed with his own speed.

Boxer galloped steadily, clearing the gate, three dykes, a barbed-wire fence. And now the railway lay ahead and William thought, he'll turn for the crossing and I can cut him off, and he swung Boxer towards the road twenty metres away. Leon saw the bank ahead, topped by wire. He knew the line lay below. He wanted to turn but he couldn't stop Flaming Prince, his long thoroughbred stride was eating up the ground, his neck was stretched forward, his jaws set. Leon wasn't frightened. In an odd way he was beyond fear. He couldn't remember whether the line was electrified or not, and he didn't know whether it could kill. He tried all the tricks he had been taught to stop a runaway horse – crossing his hands, trying to turn a circle, pulling one hand up and over the neck. But the more he pulled, the faster Flaming Prince galloped, and now he had almost reached the line, and he started to laugh and shout, "You won't catch me now." And he remembered something he'd heard once. "One crowded hour of glorious life is worth an age without a name . . ." And in a strange way he was happy, happier than he had been for months.

The red lights were flashing at the crossing, which meant a train was coming, and William started to yell, "Stop, Leon! There's a train coming. Stop . . ."

But Flaming Prince was still galloping, with Leon sitting on top riding as though he hadn't a care in the world. He wants to die, thought William, he doesn't care.

He could hear the train coming now and he pushed Boxer with his legs, and now he was going faster than he had ever gone before, but it wasn't fast enough. He was neck and neck with the train now, and he started to wave and shout, "Stop! Please stop! There's a horse on the line." And passengers waved back. He thought he heard a child's voice call, "Ride him, Cowboy." And a boy of his own age made a V-sign. And then the red lights had stopped flashing, and Flaming Prince was over the wire fence and going down the bank, and William couldn't see him any more and the train wasn't stopping. For an awful moment William thought of what he would see when the train and horse met, and he shut his eyes. He heard the train tearing away at tremendous speed and he started to pray, "God, don't let it happen, please God."

It seemed the longest moment of his life. But when he opened his eyes again. Leon was over the bank on the other side, waving and laughing and the train was gone.

Daylight had come now and they were still galloping. Boxer was drenched with sweat and they had lost ground – fifty metres at least; William trotted through the crossing and saw that a man was delivering milk and an old woman was walking a dog. Then he was galloping again, over another dyke, over a fence, across thick clogging plough that knocked the heart out of a horse and strained his tendons, towards a distant wood and he knew he wasn't gaining on Leon, not a metre, not a centimetre, just holding his own, and he wondered how many miles they had covered, and how much longer they could go on. How long would it take for Flaming Prince to crack, he wondered, to stop sobbing for breath, and could Boxer stay as long . . .? And he wondered again about Leon. What was he really like, for instance? Did anyone know? Perhaps in the end they would meet and fight it out, perhaps in the wood, and it would be a fight to death, William was sure of that.

Marvin and Natasha had reached Deep Wood Farm, but the fire engines were there before them. Most of the straw was burnt.

"It wasn't even insured. I didn't even have time to insure it," said Mr Gaze.

"And William's gone after Leon. We don't know why. We suppose it's an old vendetta come alive again," said Mrs Gaze. "But it seems a funny time to gallop off, just when we needed him."

"There's more to it than that," said William's father. "I have my suspicions."

Marvin still felt drunk and Natasha had started

to shiver because she had seen, quite near the fire, a little silver pocket knife which belonged to her brother. She dismounted and picked it up.

"Your brother was here before William, but he didn't wake us and William wouldn't have gone after him without a reason. He's not that daft," said Mr Gaze, with a knowing look on his face. "Ah, here come the police."

Natasha was crying now and she felt cold to the marrow of her bones. She remembered things Leon had done long ago as a little boy, like burning cushions and setting fire to her favourite doll's hair. They had seemed so pointless, just as the burnt straw was pointless. And she didn't understand.

William's father was saying, "They went that way. Now where's that little penknife? Here, give it here, Natasha. It's evidence. That's why I left it here, as evidence."

And the police were getting into their cars, talking into their walkie-talkies.

Marvin didn't understand either, and his mind was foggy with drink. "I think I'm going home," he said. "I hope you don't mind." No one took any notice.

William's mother was lamenting that William had no hat on his head, and Natasha was weeping. And Mr Gaze was calling. "You catch him. Bring him back here. Let me tell him what I think of him," waving to the patrol cars racing away, their sirens howling.

Amanda had stopped to rest Jack. He had only three shoes on his hoofs now and was beginning to go lame. She could see the fire engines at Deep

Wood Farm and had heard the police sirens. She thought, it's all over now. It's burnt. And she wondered where Leon and William were and why she hadn't seen a sign of them anywhere. And she wondered how the Gazes would manage without the straw, and why the arsonist had been to them twice . . . She felt very tired and she thought, it's morning now and I shall never be ready for school. I can't even remember where my clean socks are and I've forgotten to do my holiday homework and old squashed-nose Cheepers will be furious. Then she thought, perhaps Mum will let me stay at home, just this once. After all, something has happened, and even if I've been useless, probably Leon has done something marvellous and that will count, because we are all part of the same Patrol. And then, as daylight came, she saw two horses crossing the landscape, going slowly as tired horses do, with their necks stretched out, but still galloping and the riders on top were leaning forward, going with their horses, riding as though they had been galloping for hours. One was a grey, the other a bay and there was nearly half a mile between them.

Leon had heard the police sirens and was heading for the wood. He felt like a hunted fox, but it wasn't a bad feeling, because he wasn't frightened; in a strange way he was beyond fear; or perhaps it was simply that exhaustion had dulled his senses. He wasn't really thinking anyway, just galloping, and Flaming Prince wasn't pulling any more. The plough was dragging at his legs, slowing him down. He was tired now, and his breath was laboured, his sides clogged with mud and sweat.

"Just make the wood, old fellow," Leon said. "Then you can rest and get your breath."

There was one more dyke to jump between them and the wood, straight out of the thick, clinging plough on to clean golden stubble. It was a wide, deep dyke with a bit of a bank on the landing side. Leon pushed Flaming Prince with his legs; he knew he needed impulsion behind him, a great thrust from his quarters if he was to lift himself out of the plough and clear the dyke, but there wasn't any thrust left. Flaming Prince took off, game to the end, but his hind legs hardly left the plough and the next moment they were both in the dyke. Flaming Prince's nose hit the bank on the other side and he seemed to fold up. Leon's shoulder hit the far bank too, with one leg still stuck under Flaming Prince's stomach. Leon yelled, "Get off it, you fool," and hit Flaming Prince with his gun and the horse gave a great sigh and rolled over and then Leon's leg was free and Flaming Prince was lying on his side, not breathing any more.

Leon leapt up then and started to run towards the wood, and he thought, Flaming Prince had broken his neck and I shall never have another horse like him. What a terrible night it's been.

Amanda saw them fall and leapt on to Jack and galloped towards the wood, beating him with the reins. . .

William stopped at the dyke and looked at Flaming Prince. Boxer snorted and rolled his eyes. William, being a farmer's son, knew a dead animal when he saw one, but seeing poor Flaming Prince crumpled in the dyke still sent a shiver down his spine. He wanted to stop and cover him up, to say, "I'm sorry it ended this way. It wasn't meant to." But there was still Leon to be caught. So he turned

Boxer round and rode him back and said, "Don't do the same. Jump big, or you'll be dead too."

He rode him with all his strength and then they were over the dyke and galloping towards the wood, and the stubble was light to cross after the plough, and William could feel Boxer finding new heart.

The wood was thick and dark and very wet. William left Boxer standing outside and crawled through a wire fence and shouted, "You had better give yourself up, Leon. The police will get you in the end. There's no point in killing me. You don't want to be had for murder."

"Flaming Prince is dead and I've got a gun. I don't care what happens to me, but I hate you, William. I always have. You have everything I haven't got . . ."

They could hear police sirens in the distance now. They are like packs of howling wolves after their prey, thought William. I wish I wasn't here. The night was long gone now and it was another Monday. Quite near, tractors were starting up; life was going on as though nothing terrible was happening – it made William feel small and insignificant. School must be starting now without me, he thought, and imagined his empty desk. "What have I got which you haven't, Leon?" he called. "I'm just a farmer's boy – remember?"

"Don't come any nearer or I'll shoot," shouted Leon.

I'm not going to run this time, thought William. He ached all over and his knees seemed stuck in a riding position. He couldn't see Leon, but he knew where he was by his voice. He crawled through the undergrowth, scratching his face and hands. He wondered where the others were now, mostly Amanda, and he thought, this is the end of the Patrol, it can't go on any more.

He stood up at last, and could see Leon leaning against a tree, muddy and dishevelled, one arm held at a strange angle as though it was injured. And suddenly, he was sorry for him, and all the Merriots, and he thought again, why did he do it?

Leon had seen him and he started to yell again, "Don't come any nearer or I'll shoot." And then William was running towards him, his head low, making for his legs. Leon pulled the trigger, but there weren't any bullets in the gun, and now William was holding on to his legs, pulling him down. Another second and they were both rolling on the ground and Leon was hitting William with his gun, yelling, "You deserve it. My God, you do."

In between the blows, William managed to yell, "Why did you do it?" And Leon stopped hitting him and said, "I burnt ours too. You didn't know that, did you? I was very clever because I was miles away when it happened. I did some experiments first. I arranged things, so that it would be at least an hour before the flames started."

"But why?"

"And it was an hour and a half exactly. I timed it. And no one even suspected me. What a joke it was, even the police didn't suspect me. I got my own back there, all right."

"On whom?"

"On my dear father, who beats me. His father beat him, so he beats me. And as for you, do you remember last season, out hunting, when you pushed me out of the way at the brook? Do you think a Merriot is pushed out of the way by

anyone? I've got my own back now, haven't I?"

"I don't remember," William said. "But please Leon, let's go home. Your horse is dead, and it's another day. We're both exhausted . . ."

"I'm not going home," Leon replied. "I'm on the run now, I shall go to South America."

All William's rage had gone. He felt completely exhausted, mentally as much as physically. Leon was still holding the gun over his head. But he could hear other noises now – Boxer neighing, voices approaching, and people. Then Leon started to run again, like a hunted animal, and William thought of hunting and wished he was chasing a fox instead of Leon.

Amanda saw Boxer and dismounted. She tied Jack to a wire fence and ran towards the wood. Boxer neighed and she started to shout, "Stop fighting, remember the rules of the Patrol. Leon, William is in control. You must do what he tells you." But no one answered. "Stop!" she yelled, "these stupid vendettas are hopeless. It's Monday, another day, and William's straw is all burnt. Please stop." And slowly her voice became a wail and at the same moment rain started to fall.

Leon had reached the other side of the wood now and he could see the road lined with police cars. Policemen with dogs were descending on the wood, the dogs straining at their leashes. He wasn't afraid because he knew that the Merriots had faced worse things than dogs and policemen. His father had told him many times how his great-grandfather had died of thirst in the desert, fighting for his Queen and country, and how his grandfather had died in the trenches in the Great

War and his great-great-great-grandfather had died in the Wars of the Roses. And what were dogs and policemen compared with that? He felt as though he had been reared for this very moment, as he turned back and came face to face with William again. He yelled, "Get out of my way," but William was ready for another fight now. He used a rugby tackle, grabbing Leon round the legs and then they were both on the ground, and Leon started hitting William with his gun again. William rolled himself up in a ball and then spun round, blood running down his pullover, and hit back with his fists. And now Amanda had reached them and was screaming "Stop it! Please stop!"

She found a piece of wood and tried to hit Leon, but hit William instead, and suddenly the leaves on the ground were red with blood. She started to scream, "Help!" and the next second the police were there pulling Leon away, standing him up, putting handcuffs on him, while William stood up on shaky legs, saying, "It's only my nose bleeding."

"Have we got the right one?" a policeman asked. And Amanda said, "Yes," and started to cry because she had never seen anything so sad as Leon in handcuffs.

William looked at Leon and said, "I'm sorry."

And Leon said, "It doesn't matter. I'm sick of being at home, sick of school, sick of exams sick of being a Merriot. I shall enjoy prison."

And one of the policemen smiled and said, "You sound pretty sick to me. Come on. We'll give you some breakfast at the station. What about you, son? Your eye looks as though it needs a stitch or two above it." He was staring at William, so William said, "I have to take my horse home," and turned away because he couldn't bear to look at Leon a moment longer. "His horse is dead," he added. "I'll get Dad to send the knacker's van."

"He won't go to prison," said one of the policemen, patting Amanda on the shoulder. "He'll be all right. But what about you?"

"I'm all right. I'm going with William," replied Amanda.

Amanda and William walked through the wood together and suddenly everything seemed very quiet, with nothing but the rain falling through the trees.

"Why did he do it?" asked Amanda.

"I don't know. Too much pressure, I suppose," William answered. She was still crying, so he lent her his handkerchief.

The horses were waiting in the rain. Boxer was shivering and Jack looked thinner than ever.

"I can't face the Merriots. I can't take him back," cried Amanda. "After all, I helped to catch Leon. I feel such a traitor."

"You needn't, because the police would have caught him anyway. Dad knew it was him," said William wearily, mounting and turning Boxer's head for home.

"Leave Jack with us. He'll be all right. Dad will sort it out," he said.

"I never imagined it was Leon, not for one split second, that's why it's such a shock," exclaimed Amanda, mounting.

"The Merriots are all a bit mad; they were built for another age. Life is too ordinary for people like them," William replied. He felt no bitterness now, only a great sadness.

"Flaming Prince was a good horse. It all seems so unnecessary, somehow," he added.

They had to jump the dykes again and their horses were very tired and they were wet to the skin, but it didn't matter. Nothing really mattered compared with the awfulness of the last few hours. Amanda shut her eyes when they passed Flaming Prince. And she thought, poor Natasha, she'll be so miserable. They rode at a slow trot, a kind of hound jog, and time seemed to be passing very slowly compared with the last few hours.

William's face had started to swell and his eye ached and suddenly he didn't want to talk any more.

"We had better hurry," said Amanda, "because you need an anti-tet injection." She couldn't stop shivering.

"Only within ten hours, I'm not a horse," replied William, trying to laugh, but finding that even smiling hurt him.

"And you'll need a stitch. You look awful," continued Amanda. "The swelling is growing bigger every minute."

"What happened to the others?" asked William.

"They went home ages ago."

They could see the farm now, lying among the fields. Smoke rose from the kitchen chimney and a crowd of people stood waiting at a gate, waving.

"There's Mum. Whatever is she doing here?" said Amanda, after a moment. "I'm not hurt."

"You're tired to death; at least you look it," replied William.

"It's too late for school, isn't it?" Amanda asked, still shivering.

William nodded, and that hurt his face too.

108

"If only it hadn't been Leon. If only it could have been someone really horrible, how happy we would be feeling now," Amanda said.

"Life isn't that easy."

William's father was opening the gate now, beckoning them in. Pete was there too, and their mothers and two strangers in suits. The fire was out and there was wet, charred straw all over the yard, and the smell of fire which William would never forget.

"There's a dead horse in the dyke. Will you send the knacker, please Dad?" William asked.

Amanda slipped to the ground. Her mother wore high heels and a long coat. "I'm taking you straight home," she said.

"We'll look after Jack," said William, staggering across the yard leading Boxer. "He'll be all right with us. Don't worry, Amanda."

She was crying again now, saying to her mother, "Why did it have to be Leon?"

William dragged off Boxer's tack. Everything seemed very far away suddenly, and his words were slurred by exhaustion. He could feel his father steering him into the house, saying. "You need a doctor, son. Come on inside. You'll be better there."

And his mother saying, "I'll put the kettle on," as she always did when anything awful happened.

And he kept saying, "I'm all right. I'm perfectly all right."

Chapter Twelve

The end of a dream

William's eye had been stitched by a doctor and his face cleaned by a nurse.

"Stay away from school and keep out of fights," the doctor said, "or it will open up again for certain."

"Will it leave a scar?" his mother wanted to know.

"Not anything you'll see. Come back in three of four days and we'll see how it is. And remember, William, *keep out of fights*."

His mother drove him home. She looked tired and strung up and nearly hit a lorry.

"No school, do you hear? And you had better give up the Patrol," she said. "Why it is always you who is beaten up, I don't know."

William wasn't really listening, because he had started to worry about Willow again.

The Merriots' Daimler was parked in the yard when they reached home. The sight of it made him feel sick suddenly.

"What are they doing here?" he asked.

"They are in the front room. We can go round

the back. You must go to bed. You haven't slept the whole night," his mother said.

"I must see the horses first."

Boxer was still in the stable. He was run up, and still covered with sweat. He was resting his off fore which was swollen. William put an arm round his neck. "I'm sorry about the night," he said. "But you stood up, you made it. There never was a horse like you." He felt the heat in the swollen tendon. He knew what it meant – a strain or sprain and weeks of rest. No hunting – no more patrolling. At this moment he was too tired to care, but later he would mind, would stand at the window of his room thinking of the days with hounds he was missing; and he would feel bitter.

"You'd better have the vet," he said, checking that Boxer had hay and water before going up the hill to look at Willow. She trotted up to meet him. Her legs were clean and unblemished, her eyes shining. "You're all right, at any rate," he said.

He knew he could sleep now; and there was only Jack still to visit, standing alone in a loose-box eating hay as though he hadn't been fed for a month. When William returned to the house, the Daimler had gone. "What did he want?" he asked.

His parents were talking in the kitchen. "Mr Merriot's going to give us what the straw and hay cost. The barns were insured," his father said.

"But it's thousands of pounds! Do you mean both lots?"

"Yes. The Merriots always pay their debts, or so Colonel Merriot says," replied his father.

"And what about Leon?"

"He wouldn't come out on bail. He said he wanted to stay where he was. They are waiting for medical reports. When he's done his sentence, he's going to be sent to an uncle in Canada. He doesn't want to go home, ever again."

"I suppose he'll be sent to an Approved School," William said. "He won't like it, but he'll keep a stiff upper lip, because he's a Merriot."

"I think I would rather be us," replied his mother. "In spite of the state of the house, we seem a lot happier."

"He's a young offender. His name won't be mentioned in court. Will you keep quiet about it, too? I know it's a lot to ask, but will you? I gave your word to Colonel Merriot,' his father asked. "You don't mind do you?"

"In exchange for the money for the hay and straw, isn't it?" asked William.

"Not exactly . . ."

"I don't want to talk aboout it anyway. It's over now," William said.

"You're going to be given a certificate or something by the police for your act of bravery over the saddle thieves," his mother told him. "Isn't that lovely?"

"I don't know –" He was going upstairs now like a wounded animal to his lair. He didn't want to talk or think any more. He just wanted to sleep . . . He was too tired to undress properly. He just took off his blood-stained pull-over, his muddy breeches and lay down, and sleep came at once, blotting out everything.

Amanda broke down when she reached home. She thought she would never stop crying. "It was so awful, and Flaming Prince is dead. He is, really, Mum, and he was such a lovely horse. And what about Natasha, Mum? Do you think I should ring her up? She must be so miserable. How could Leon do it – be part of the Patrol and the arsonist as well? And we never knew, never suspected him, at least I didn't, Mum, not even when I found them fighting in the wood. Not till the police came and took him away. He burnt their straw too – all because he hated his father. Dad annoys me sometimes, but I would never do that."

"Darling, it's over now. You need to sleep, have a hot drink and then pop into bed."

"I nearly killed Jack," cried Amanda, walking up and down the living room, leaving footprints on the lush fitted carpet. "He had lost a shoe and I beat him with the reins."

"It's all over darling . . ."

"And what about school? I can't miss today. It's a terribly important day. We were going to be told what classes we are in for what lessons. I must go to school. Where are my things?"

"It's nearly twelve o'clock. By the time you get there, darling, school will be over."

"I've made a mess of everything, haven't I?" cried Amanda, collapsing on to a sofa. "I'm a failure."

Natasha was on her way to school. For the first time in her life she was glad to be going. Her father had brought her a first-class ticket and she sat alone in her carriage, feeling miserable. She still couldn't believe that the night had actually happened; her mind couldn't accept what her father had told her and she couldn't stop weeping for Flaming Prince, who was only five. Nanny had packed her clothes. Her mother had given her fifty pounds. "Buy yourself something pretty with it," she had said. As though buying something pretty would make her forget. And everyone seemed to be looking at her when she changed trains at Bletchley. Her father had told her not to mention Leon, not ever again. But she knew that would be impossible. She would write to him wherever he was sent. She had been brought up to believe that "blood is thicker than water" and she had no intention of forgetting it now. She thought, I'll miss him. He was crazy in many ways but such fun. No one has ever been as much fun as Leon. School friends were getting on to the train now, and she tried to compose her face, but she knew Flaming Prince was dead and every time she thought about it, she cried and no sooner had her friends seen her than they started saying, "What is it, Natasha? What's happened?" And she could only say, "Nothing. Nothing at all," because, like William, she was sworn to secrecy.

Marvin had slept for five hours, but now he was up and his mother was furious about the state Skinflint was in. "Just look at him," she bellowed. "His legs are swollen, he's filthy and he looks half starved. What have you been doing to him, for pity's sake?"

"Nothing much. I told you William's straw was burnt again." Marvin had an awful hangover. "But I don't know who did it."

"Well I do, and you're not to breathe a word. Colonel Merriot has been on the phone. He's terribly upset. It was Leon all along."

"Leon! But he was in the Patrol. He was on our side," protested Marvin.

114

"Mum's the word," said his mother, putting her finger to her lips. "But to go back to Skinflint. You didn't even rug him up. He could have got pneumonia, and then think of the vet bills . . ."

"But his own straw was burnt. Did he burn that too?"

"Yes, he did."

"But how? How did he do it? It just doesn't seem like him. It makes him into a traitor and the Merriots are so proud."

"He must be a bit unhinged, dear. It's his age. He will be all right in a year or two. Not to worry. And remember, not a word to anyone."

"Won't we have to give evidence?"

"Not if he pleads guilty."

"It's such a surprise," said Marvin, sitting down with his head in his hands. "Did he start all the other fires too?"

"Yes, his parents have been in London and Nanny, who is very old, stopped noticing whether he was in or out. It's a terrible thing," replied his mother.

"Who will have Flaming Prince?"

"I wondered that, because he would have suited you, but he broke his neck trying to jump a dyke, poor animal. So he's dead."

"Please don't let's talk about it any more. I wish I could go to school. Is it really too late?" Marvin said. He was crying now. He didn't know whether it was for Leon or Flaming Prince. He had admired them both.

"Yes. I've cooked you some lunch, come and have it . . ." His mother led the way into the dining room. Marvin blew his nose and wiped his eyes. He had started to feel sick again.

"I've made ever such a nice lunch," his mother said, as though that could heal his anguish. "Look, there's chicory, and tomatoes from the greenhouse, and cold beef, and there's your favourite pudding to follow."

"I've always admired Leon so much," Marvin said. "That's why I'm so upset. I always wanted to be like him, and now look what's happened. It's all so muddling. I still can't understand what made him do it."

"Don't try to. We may never know," replied his mother.

"But there must be a reason," shouted Marvin.

"I want you to groom Skinflint after you've eaten, Marvin, and then clean his tack. His box needs cleaning out too. You've been neglecting things, dear. Everything is in the most ghastly mess," said his mother, talking as though the night had never taken place. "And it must be put straight before your father comes home."

"Yes, it is in a ghastly mess, with Leon in prison and Flaming Prince dead. And what about William and Amanda and Natasha?" cried Marvin, pushing away his lunch. "And what about the Patrol?"

"I don't know about Amanda, William and Natasha, but I think the Patrol should die a convenient death. It was a bad idea from start to finish," his mother answered.

"But it worked," cried Marvin. "It caught the arsonist, and it caught the men stealing the Doyles' saddles; at least William did. You can't say that isn't success."

William was awake now. He could smell onions cooking downstairs. He sat up in bed and looked at

116

his alarm clock and saw that it was seven o'clock. He put on his transistor radio and decided it was evening, not morning, and he thought, that's that – no more Patrol, no more Boxer for months. Nobody will want to ride out again after last night. The Patrol had better die, like Flaming Prince. Besides, who is there left?

He got up and looked at himself in the mirror above his cluttered chest of drawers and didn't like what he saw. Smelling the onions made him hungry and he dressed hurriedly, hurting his eye by pulling a polo-necked sweater over his head. He thought, tomorrow I'll ring up Marvin and Amanda and tell them the Patrol's over. I'll thank them for belonging and tear up the constitution. There's no point in going on. We're all too battered and too tired and everybody left in it is too young, except for me.

His parents were sitting in the kitchen, eating. "I'll get yours. It's in the oven. How do you feel, son?" asked his mother.

"The same as before."

"You won't be right for a bit," his father said. "But I'm proud of you."

"Leon crossed the railway line. He jumped down and out. It was terrifying," said William, remembering. "He's got courage, and his horse could certainly jump."

He sat down and started to eat. "The train could have killed them both." He was beginning to feel better. "What am I going to do with Boxer lame?" he asked.

"We'll find you something in the market next week. They're dirt cheap – a young 'un with a bit of blood about him," his father said. "Until then you can have old Mulberry. He could do with some work."

117

"Phone," said his mother. "It's Amanda, for you, William."

"How are you?" he said, picking up the phone.

"I'm all right. What about Jack?"

"He's improving. He needs shoeing though –"

"You're telling me. I rang up to ask you if you could come here on Friday after school for a meeting," she said.

"To wind up the Patrol?" he asked.

"To discuss it anyway. I'm asking Marvin; there's no one else because Natasha's back at school. She went this morning," Amanda said.

"What time then?"

"Half past five, for tea."

"See you then . . ." He put down the receiver thinking, it's the end of a dream, just a dream which didn't work out.

"What was that about?"

"We're going to end the Patrol."

"I'm sorry," said his mother. "But you've got your exams to think about."

"And the nights are drawing in," said his father.

They didn't understand, they never had. He had imagined a flag, a great band of them riding forth, singing, a power of good in the land, a sort of crusade, even a reason for living. And now it had come to three of them winding it all up like winding wool on a chair. He wasn't hungry any more. "I'm going out to tea on Friday," he said. "I shan't be late." And he wished Friday would never come. His father looked at his face and said, "You'll have your new horse to school. We'll buy you a good one. You won't have time for anything else, not with the dark evenings coming along."

Chapter Thirteen

We've got to help

William thought Friday would never come. He moped at home, getting on his parents' nerves. On Wednesday, Maggy's mother came to take Jack back to the Merriots. She was a tall angular woman, with long, dark hair. William thought she resembled a crow. She drank coffee in the kitchen and discussed the Merriots and their way of life. And William went away and rode Mulberry, because he couldn't bear to listen.

Mulberry was large and roan, with a roman nose and large plodding feet. He was a very kind horse, who could open a gate almost on his own, and always knew the shortest way home. But he wasn't Boxer. William thought about his next horse. He wanted another grey, something well bred like Flaming Prince, but wiser and kinder.

He lunged Willow to keep her fit and then Suzy. His eye didn't hurt any more and the swelling was going down.

When he returned to the house, Maggy's mother had gone.

"I hope the old crow's going to feed up poor Jack," William said. "He's still in awful shape."

"They may be leaving. Leon's behaviour has broken his father's heart, apparently," said William's mother.

"I bet . . ." He didn't want to talk about Leon and he didn't want to think about the Patrol before Friday. He ran upstairs into his room and slammed the door. He felt as though his own heart was breaking, though he couldn't have said why. Later he went out and looked at Boxer's tendon, which was still swollen, and knew that he wouldn't be fit to ride for six months at least.

On Thursday he saw the doctor again who said, "You've kept out of fights then? Good boy," as though the fight had been a sort of game. "We'll leave the stitches in a bit longer though, and you keep on behaving yourself. No fights, no tearing about on motor bikes," the doctor said.

"I don't have a motor bike. I ride horses," answered William. "And I'm not in the habit of fighting. Anyway, I'm too young for motor bikes."

The rest of the day dragged by. Rain fell in torrents all afternoon and the yard was like a marsh. Pete wandered about with a sack across his shoulders, and the farmhouse roof started to leak.

Then, at last, it was Friday. William stayed in bed until lunch time, with his transistor on full blast, trying not to think about the evening. After lunch he watched television, and then suddenly it was time to go to Amanda's, and he felt all on edge. He put on an old waterproof and rode his bike, and the sky was full of dark dancing clouds, and a breeze fanned his face. He arrived too early, and Amanda's mother led the way into the sitting room and said, "No dirty marks, please. The chair covers have just been to the cleaners, and watch your boots. The walls are clean too."

He sat down on a yellow sofa feeling big and untidy and ill at ease, and Amanda's mother said. "The others will be here in a minute," and stared at his boots.

There was nothing to look at in the room, just four walls, empty furniture and velvet curtains. William would have liked to look out of the window for the others, but he was afraid his boots would leave marks on the carpet, so he stayed where he was, pitying Amanda. He could hear the chink of cups coming from the kitchen and he thought, the tea will be dainty, lots of little sandwiches and paper napkins. Then Amanda burst into the room shrieking, "You're early. But it doesn't matter. How are the horses?" She was wearing school clothes and looked clean and tidy.

"Okay," William said, suddenly shy.

Two minutes later Marvin arrived and Amanda's mother brought in tea, putting plates of food on the coffee tables scattered about the room. "You can pour out," she said, looking at Amanda. "And don't make crumbs any of you. I know how you young people are nowadays – no manners."

"I'm sorry about Mum," Amanda said when she had left the room. "She's got a bit of a mania about cleanliness."

William sat on the edge of the sofa waiting for someone to speak. After a time he said, "We *are* attending a funeral, aren't we? We are winding up the Patrol. Isn't that why we are here?"

"I can't go on. I'm sorry," Amanda answered. "It isn't me. It's my parents."

"Nor can I. They don't want Skinflint dead, or me bashed up like you, William," Marvin said.

"So we think we ought to end it formally," Amanda said.

"I don't know why. Why couldn't it just die a natural death, or rot away?" replied William bitterly.

"It's our parents, it isn't us," Amanda replied. "Really, William."

"Okay," he said. "I've brought the constitution. Can we have a sort of cremation when we've finished tea?" His bitterness alarmed them, while deep inside himself he was near to tears.

"It was formed to catch the arsonist and we've caught him. Isn't that enough?" asked Amanda.

"It was formed to be a power of good in the land. To ride forth on all sorts of errands," replied William.

Amanda passed him an iced cake in a frilly paper case and he thought, they don't belong to my world. They are townspeople really. Leon was the one with courage. The cake tasted like sawdust with a faint lemon flavour. The tea was china tea in delicate flowered cups. Amanda's mother came in to draw the curtains, though it wasn't nearly dark outside. "Are you looking after your guests?" she asked Amanda, looking at William's boots, which he now saw had straw on them.

"Yes, she is," replied Marvin.

Leon wouldn't have given up, thought William. I wonder where he is now. He took the constitution from his pocket and read it through.

"We can't burn it here, because there isn't any grate," he said, looking round the room.

"There isn't a fireplace in the whole bungalow," said Amanda. "We have under-floor heating and an electric cooker, and you can't burn it on that. Mum would be furious."

She's furious anyway, thought William, looking at his boots.

"We had better take it outside then, but let's finish tea first," suggested Marvin, helping himself to another cake.

"Dad won't like the ashes in the garden," said Amanda.

"The wind will carry them away. Or shall I make a coffin for them?" asked William. Marvin and Amanda didn't seem like friends any more. William wanted to go home and relax. He wanted the cremation over and done with. I shall be the only one who mourns, he thought.

But now the telephone was ringing. "It's all right. Mum will answer it in the bedroom. I expect it's for Dad," Amanda said, piling their empty teacups on to a tray. She looked different in school clothes, more ordinary, thought William.

He stood up, screwing up the constitutions in his hand. He felt slightly sick. "It was born out of fire, so it shall die by fire," he said.

"We'll burn it on the patio," announced Amanda, sounding worried. 'Dad can't object to that. I'll get some matches. I didn't mean this meeting to be like this at all. It was just to be a gathering. You've made everything seem so sad, William. And you make everything seem my fault." Amanda was nearly crying. "I don't really want it to end. Can't you understand? But I've got school, exams."

"Exactly," agreed Marvin.

"Telephone for you, William. It's your mother. She sounds a bit agitated. You can take it here," said Amanda's mother peering round the door.

A thousand possibilities rushed through

William's mind as he crossed the room to the telephone – his father injured in an accident, one of the horses lying with a broken leg, the house on fire, Boxer dead. When he picked up the telephone receiver his hand was shaking.

"Yes, it's me. What is it?" he asked.

"The police have just phoned. They want you to phone them," his mother said. He could feel Marvin and Amanda looking at him and he could have sworn Amanda's mother was listening through the keyhole.

"What's the matter? Is it trouble?" he asked.

A hush settled over the room. For a second he could hear nothing but his own breathing. "They'll tell you what it is. The number to ring is . . ."

Amanda handed him a piece of paper and a pencil. He heard a small click and knew that her mother had picked up the extension, so that she could listen in. He thought, nosey old woman, as he wrote down the number. "Come home soon," his mother said, and rang off.

"It's the police. Can I phone the station?" he asked. "Or do you want to complete the cremation first?" He felt quite calm now.

"Of course you can phone. Do you want us to leave the room? Is it private?" asked Amanda, looking worried.

"I don't know, but you can stay," he answered. He dialed a wrong number and a woman kept saying, "Is that you, Sid? You're late ringing. I've been waiting in all afternoon."

He tried again and this time it was the police station and he said, "It's William Gaze here," and how his hand was shaking again, and he was so nervous he could hardly hear anything.

"The Chief Inspector wondered if you could help us," a voice said. "We know you have a mounted Patrol and there's a little girl lost somewhere on the marshes. We are planning a search at dawn and you, might be able to see more than the helicopters. We are having dogs of course."

He was so excited he hardly heard the rest. He heard " . . . might be calling in the Army," and "She's a disabled child and she could be anywhere."

And he said, "We'll have to box, but that's all right."

And the policeman said something about all costs being covered. And he could feel Amanda at his elbow saying, "What is it, William? What's happening."

And he knew now that the Patrol would have to go on.

He said, "I'll ring you later when I've got things organized," and he wrote down a name and a number without really knowing what he was doing before he put down the phone.

"We've got a job," he said, turning to the others. "There's a child lost in the marshes, a little girl of six. We've got to help. You can have Suzy, Amanda, and I will have Mulberry. We had better ring up the Doyles, and Maggy and Saskia, and hire a box for them." While he was talking he was smoothing out the constitution between his hands, imagining them riding forth in the dawn, thinking, no one can object to us searching for a little girl. And Amanda's mother was in the room now, saying, "You must go, Amanda. It's an errand of mercy. I'm not objecting, darling. Poor little mite."

And Marvin was putting on his school blazer, saying, "I'm going home to get ready."

"I'll ring you up when things are fixed," said William, looking at his dirty boots without really seeing them, knowing that such things didn't matter any more.

"I'll catch up the horses and phone the others. Goodbye," he said.

And the constitution of the Pony Patrol was still there in his pocket, alive and kicking. And, mounting his bike, he thought, if the police need us, we must be a success. We must be known *and* respected.

He wanted to burst into song, to yell to the world, "The Pony Patrol lives on!" but the thought of the little girl sobered him. He imagined her alone, while night came down like a curtain blotting out everything. A little girl, with fair hair, lost and scared, wet and hungry. He started to make plans, to imagine them un-boxing horses with desolate land all about them, going forth to greater glory.

But whether she was ever found and what actually happened, belongs to another book.

PONY PATROL

The Pony Patrol – a team of young riders whose sworn aim is to patrol the countryside on horseback, watching, searching and protecting the peace of the land.

Follow the adventures of the Pony Patrol riders in Christine Pullein-Thompson's gripping series of books.

Pony Patrol	£2.99 ☐
Pony Patrol S.O.S.	£2.99 ☐

Available in 1992:

Pony Patrol Fights Back
Pony Patrol and the Mystery Horse